FREESIAS AND FOUL PLAY

PORT DANBY COZY MYSTERY #12

LONDON LOVETT

WILD FOX PRESS

CHAPTER 1

The familiar chime of the bell on the door was followed by Lola. This morning she had my pet crow perched uncharacteristically on her shoulder. The cold snap, a mid-spring surprise, curled its frosty tendrils around the shop before the door swung shut. I pulled the edges of my sweater closer to ward off the chill that had come with my scratchy sore throat (another mid-spring surprise).

Kingston stayed securely on Lola's shoulder and would probably stay there until coaxed away from the love of his life by one of Elsie's peanut butter dog treats, the second love of his life. I fell somewhere after Lola, the treats, perching in one of the town square's pine trees and rummaging through crumbly beach picnic leftovers with his adopted family, the Port Danby seagulls. But then who was I? I only saved the bird from certain death and provided him with a secure, warm home and all the hardboiled eggs he could eat. Lola merely had to smile his direction, and his beady black eyes glittered with stars and hearts. Not literally, of course, but they were easy to imagine with the way he looked at her.

With a huff, Lola hopped up onto the stool at my work island. "I'm reliving my worst childhood nightmare." One thing I discovered early on about Lola was that she rarely wasted time with mundane greetings like hello and good morning. She usually just jumped into whatever was on her mind for the day.

I pushed a yellow rose into the arrangement I was creating for a birthday gift. "You never told me having a crow land on your shoulder was your worst childhood nightmare."

"What?" She glanced over at Kingston. They were nose to beak for a moment, then Kingston shyly turned to stare casually out the window. "No, not Kingston. By the way, if you're wondering why we're together, like pirate and friend today, it's because your bird now feels perfectly free to trot into the antique shop every time the opportunity presents itself. He spent the morning strutting along my front counter, leaving talon prints on my newly polished glass. Mrs. Churchill, from over on Dawson Grove, walked inside the shop, placed her fists on her ample hips and said, 'oh no, not you too? Does every shop owner in Port Danby have a pet crow?' I tried to explain to her that Kingston was the same crow she saw in the flower shop, but she talked right over me going on about how the crows destroy her vegetable gardens and scoff at the scarecrow she spent hours sewing and stuffing with straw."

"I guess we can conclude that Mrs. Churchill, like our dear mayor, is not a fan of crows." I pulled a long strand of silky blue ribbon off the spool.

"My sweater is not a fan of his talons." Lola pointed discretely at Kingston. "Maybe a treat or something, so I can rid myself of the sharp-clawed hitchhiker."

I chuckled as I reached for the treat can. "Sorry about that. You should have made him fly over." I cleared my rough throat and dug out a treat.

Kingston hopped off Lola's shoulder, plucked the treat from my fingers and flew across to his window perch to enjoy it.

Lola tilted her head at me. "Why do you sound as if you've been screaming and singing along at a concert?"

I swallowed a sip of my tea and scrunched my nose. "That sure got cold fast." I put the cup down. "I woke up with a sore throat."

Lola leaned back, apparently out of germ range. "Don't give it to me. My colds always end with two weeks of an annoying cough." The door opened and Ryder walked inside to start his shift. Lola pointed at him. "And don't give it to him either because then I'm guaranteed to get it."

Ryder pulled off his coat. "Don't give me what?"

"I've been instructed, actually commanded, not to give you my cold." I tied a bow around the vase in front of me.

Ryder looked properly sympathetic. "You're sick, boss? You poor thing. I'll go down to Franki's later and buy you some hot soup."

I lifted a brow at Lola. "See, that's how a true friend reacts when someone is sick."

Lola shrugged. "I'm a true friend, and I'm there for you when you need me, just not when you're sick. I'm selfish like that," she said with complete confidence and not an ounce of shame.

I wound up the rest of the blue ribbon. "You never told me why you were reliving your childhood's worst nightmare."

My statement caught Ryder's attention. His face snapped Lola's direction. "Did you find a spider on your toothbrush again?"

A laugh spurted from my mouth. "Wait, that's your worst childhood nightmare? A spider on your toothbrush?"

Lola shrugged. "Go ahead, make fun but that little spider traumatized me so badly, I refused to brush my teeth for a week."

"Yuck," Ryder and I muttered in unison.

"Thanks goodness you got over that bit of trauma," Ryder continued in the same muted tone.

"Anyhow, the spider incident wasn't my worst childhood nightmare, it was my third worst. Second place went to the time when I threw up in front of my fourth grade class while reading aloud my spring poem."

"I hope this whole conversation gets less gross." I leaned back to admire my work. The yellow roses looked amazing with puffs of dark blue hydrangeas.

Ryder nodded with approval. "That looks great."

"Thanks." I said. "So, what is number one on the list?"

"Flying monkeys," Lola said succinctly. "I just saw two of them walking out of Les's shop with mocha lattes, and they brought back all kinds of terrifying memories."

"I take it you're talking about the two actors from the traveling Oz play. I saw them handing out flyers this morning. They do look a little creepy in full costume," I noted.

"A little creepy?" Lola asked.

"What do you have against a little theater and culture?" Ryder asked. "I saw Mayor Price this morning. He is so proud of this whole *Wizard of Oz* event at the town square, you'd think he wrote the book himself. I thought the costumes were cool." He was obviously feeling a touch contrary this morning. Fortunately, Lola was too steeped in her nightmare about creepy flying monkeys to notice.

"My parents insisted I watch that stupid movie with the scary green witch, talking scarecrows and all the other horrifying characters," Lola continued. "I still remember the night well. My mom popped a big bowl of popcorn—microwave, of course. That was the extent of her cooking talents. We all sat down on the couch to watch what they insisted was one of the best movies of all time. I spent half of it with the couch pillow over my face and the other half curled up hiding behind my dad's shoulder. Needless to say, I did not come away thinking it was the best movie of all time. Frankly, I should have walked out when that wretched lady came and took Toto away. That should have been my clue that it was all going to go downhill from there."

I picked up the arrangement to put in the cooler to stay fresh. "It wasn't one of my favorite movies, but I didn't find it all that scary."

"You don't sound good, boss," Ryder said. He took the arrangement from me. "You should probably avoid refrigeration today."

"Thanks. I'm definitely feeling this cold snap in my bones."

"Well, I guess I'll head back to my shop," Lola said. "Seems I won't get any sympathy for my flying monkey phobia in here this morning."

I picked up the various stem pieces strewn on the work island. "I take it that means you're not going to opening night at the play. The whole town will be there. James and I have two seats right up front."

"She flatly refused when I asked her," Ryder said as he returned from the cooler.

"Yes, and I'm sticking with that refusal. I don't need to start all those weird dreams again." Lola shivered at the memory.

"Boy, that movie really traumatized you," I said, trying to sound sympathetic but unable to completely suppress my amusement. Lola was one of those brave, devil-may-care people who rarely let things frighten her. Whereas, I lost my marbles whenever a power outage turned out the lights. It was nice to find some holes in her armor.

Lola, knowing me too well, sensed that I was wholly entertained by her flying monkey phobia. "Again, it seems I came to the wrong place for solace and support this morning." She hopped off the stool, but Ryder interrupted her march to the door with a brief hug and kiss.

"I think it's adorable that you're afraid of actors dressed like monkeys," he said. "And if you need me to come save you from them, just text."

She stared up at him. "Mockery camouflaged by a sweet kiss is still mockery. I'm going to leave the shop of flower arranging meanies and head to my own safe zone where I won't be ridiculed." She headed toward the door.

"Thanks for bringing my bird back," I said. "And feel free to shoo him out of your store anytime."

"Why would I do that? Kingston loves me unconditionally, unlike my best friend and boyfriend." With that, she swept out of the store.

Ryder and I had one more chuckle as we watched her stop at the curb and look up and down the street (apparently for flying monkeys) before dashing across and inside the antique store as if someone was chasing her.

"Poor thing," I mused. "She is really freaked out by those monkeys."

Ryder couldn't hold back a grin. "Guess I've picked out my next Halloween costume."

CHAPTER 2

I'd just finished cleaning up from the birthday arrangement when an unfamiliar couple walked into the shop. The woman, a petite thirty-something with curly brown hair and large brown eyes, was clinging possessively to the man's arm. He looked about the same age as the woman but with straw blond hair and wide-set hazel eyes. He walked with sort of a clumsy galumph as they approached the counter. Their matching t-shirts were emblazoned with the words Auburn Theater Group.

I smiled broadly. "How exciting. You two are with the traveling play. I've got tickets for opening night. Can't wait to see it."

They both grinned proudly. "We're looking forward to a packed house," the man said. His voice was hoarse like mine, only I doubted his was caused by a sore throat. He pried his arm from the woman's grasp and tapped his chest. "I'm Gordon Houser. I play Scarecrow."

I smiled again. "Even more exciting to meet the actual cast members." I turned my pleased expression toward the woman. She seemed a little less inclined to introduce herself.

"Constance Jeeves," she said quietly. "I have a variety of parts, including a Munchkin and a flying monkey." She listed her character parts quickly.

"How wonderful. My friend and I were just having a lively conversation about flying monkeys. It seems two of your fully costumed cast members were hopping about town this morning handing out flyers for the play."

"Yes, that was at the mayor's request," Gordon interjected. He squinted, trying to remember his name. "Mayor Pierce?"

"Mayor Price," I corrected. "Yes, he's very excited to have the play come to our small, humble town."

Ryder came out from the back holding a vase filled with red roses.

Constance perked right up to her tiptoes to get a better look at them. "Look, Gordon, that's what I want. They'll look perfect on my dressing table." She turned to him with shiny, adoring eyes. "Then I can think of you while I'm getting ready."

Gordon seemed less enthusiastic about having to shell out money for roses. "Red roses are always the most expensive. How about some nice chrysanthemums?"

Constance sat back sharply on her heels and put on an impressive pout. "Red roses show you love me."

Gordon was saved from the awkward moment by his phone. He pulled it from his pocket and looked at it. His face flushed lightly.

"Is that Susana again?" Constance asked with dramatic exasperation.

"Uh, yeah, it's Susana. Excuse me for a second." Gordon walked over to the window and noticed Kingston for the first time. He decided to take a few steps away from the large, black bird to send a return text.

Constance turned to me. "Our director is so needy. I don't know how she manages to put on a successful production." She was not hindered by Gordon's lack of enthusiasm for the red roses. "How much for a dozen of the red roses?" she asked, apparently determined to have them.

"They're thirty dollars a dozen or three dollars a stem," I said.

She bit her lip in thought, then glanced across the room. Gordon was still deep in a text conversation. He wasn't paying an ounce of attention to his friend, and she became instantly irritated.

"Oh my gosh, just tell Susana to deal with her problem alone," she snapped.

Gordon sent off one last text and pushed the phone into his pocket. He returned to the counter. My own take on his expression was that he was feeling guilty about something but then what did I know about actors and their everyday facial emotions.

"What did she want?" Constance asked. It seemed like a perfectly reasonable follow-up question, but it threw Gordon off his stride.

"Who? Oh, you mean Su—Susana," he stuttered over the name. A long drawn out shrug followed. "You know Susie, she's always worrying about silly things."

Constance swallowed the explanation without further questioning. I wasn't entirely sure Gordon was telling the truth about any of it.

"They're three dollars each or you can save money if you buy me a dozen." Constance was back on her flower order.

"Three dollars each?" he asked with big eyes. "I could just pick you some out of a garden."

Constance was irritated and not just because of Gordon's lack of eagerness for the rose purchase. She groaned in frustration as she shoved back the sleeve of her coat, exposing a red, splotchy rash. She rubbed it several times. "This rash is getting worse."

I peered over the counter at her arm. "Wow, that looks miserable. Food allergy?" I asked.

"It's from the makeup for the flying monkey costume. They

cake the stuff on to make it look like fur. I've got splotches like this all over." Constance pushed her sleeve back down. The rash complaint didn't seem to soften up Gordon's stance on the roses. She blinked her oversized eyes at him. "It sure would be nice to have some flowers to brighten my mood."

It was hard to understand how Gordon allowed himself to be led into the flower shop in the first place. He finally relented and pulled out his wallet with a frustrated sigh. "We'll take six roses." Constance opened her mouth to protest, but he stopped her with a fatherly head tilt. "I think we should spend the rest of the money on a salve for that rash. After all, there's a dress rehearsal this afternoon, and Susie called for full costume. You'll be stuck in that makeup all night."

"I suppose you're right, Gordy. What would I do without you?"

I nodded to Ryder and pulled out my receipt pad as he set to work plucking six, lush red roses from the container to arrange in a small bouquet.

I grabbed a pen. "So, you're doing a dress rehearsal before the opening show?" I asked. "That seems tiring."

"That's because our silly director forgot to schedule the dress rehearsal," Constance explained. "Now, we're all going to be frazzled, and our costumes won't be fresh for opening night. But don't worry, the play will be wonderful," she added briskly.

"I'm sure of it," I said.

Gordon's phone beeped again. He walked over to the window, but this time he paused to admire Kingston before returning a text.

"Seriously," Constance said in exasperation. "Now what? She should start sharing her salary with you." Constance turned back to me. "He's so smart. That's why the director always needs his assistance. We've been together for two years." She leaned closer to lower her voice. "I'm just waiting for him to work up the courage to propose. I can tell you if he doesn't pop the question soon, I'm going to ask him myself. I mean, who ever invented the rule that the guy has to propose? Right?"

Ryder handed her the roses. "I suppose the same guy who made up the rule that men have to buy the flowers." He winked and walked away, leaving that little chunk of sarcasm hovering in the rose scented air. My normally gentlemanly assistant was definitely in a mood this morning.

Gordon returned to the counter to pay for the roses. He plucked the money from his wallet. "I have to ask the obvious— why is there a crow sitting in a flower shop?"

"I suppose a brightly colored parrot would be the more reasonable choice, but Kingston and I crossed paths a few years back and we've been together ever since."

"Kingston?" Constance giggled. "You named a crow?"

"Well, if he's a pet, of course he needs a name," Gordon said sharply. I wasn't going to place any bet on him popping the question soon. He seemed mostly annoyed by Constance.

I gave him the change. "I'll see you later, and good luck finding a brain."

Gordon laughed. He was a nice looking man when he smiled. "If I had a dollar for every time someone told me that."

"Then you could have bought me an entire dozen instead of six," Constance added.

Gordon had no response. The two actors walked out of the shop. Constance held the flowers in one hand and his arm in the other.

"Lola is right," Ryder spoke over my shoulder. "Those flying monkeys are scary." He walked away.

"Are you all right, Ryder?"

He glanced back over his shoulder. "Fine. Why do you ask?"

"It just seems like your mood is a little darker than usual. But maybe the cold in my head is clouding my perception."

He didn't answer at first and busied himself at the potting table.

11

"Nope, everything is fine." The way he said it assured me that things were anything *but* fine. I decided to drop the subject for the time being. I was sure I'd figure it out by the end of the day. After all, I was pretty good at solving mysteries.

CHAPTER 3

*R*yder, I'm meeting James at Franki's for lunch," I called as I headed to the door. "I should be back in an hour."

"Have a good lunch," he called back. His mood had lightened some, but that might have been more due to the rush of customers we had after this morning's red rose episode. It's hard to stay grumpy or dwell on things when you're busy selling flowers.

I pulled my hood up over my ears. The cold was slowly moving from my throat to my head. My muscles were starting to get that mushy, achy feeling that came with every cold and flu. The brisk ocean breeze carried a chill with it, which didn't help. I hunkered down in my big coat and tucked my head back under the hood. I looked like I was about to hike up a snowy hill rather than take a short spring walk to the diner.

All the icky aches and chills left me when I spotted my breathtaking Detective Briggs standing in front of the diner.

Even my smile felt weak. "There's nothing better to help clear a head cold than a picture of the world's most handsome detective standing in front of my favorite diner."

He hugged me briefly but avoided a kiss. (A smart move. I was definitely not in a kissable state of being.) "Since you've obviously never seen all the detectives in the world to make that judgment, I won't let it go to my head. However, I will accept it from the world's cutest investigative assistant." He leaned back from the hug. "And I don't have to see the rest of the world's assistants to know I'm right on that." He decided a forehead kiss wasn't too risky but frowned afterward. "You're warm," he said.

"Good, that means I'm not dead," I said wryly.

"Lacey, you should be home in bed." He opened the door to the diner.

"Nothing a bowl of Franki's minestrone soup can't cure. Besides, I'm fine. Just a little head cold."

The lunch crowd was extra boisterous, possibly a result of the cold snap that had moved into town. I'd found that just like with animals, brisk temperatures could make people more energetic. If only some of that energy had found me.

I put on a cheery smile as I slid along the vinyl seat, pretending that all was well when, in truth, the notion of climbing into my warm bed sounded more inviting with each passing minute.

Briggs reached into his pocket. "I've got two surprises for you."

"If one is that you've discovered an instant cure for the common cold, I might just get up and dance a little polka right here on Franki's tile floor."

Lines formed around his crooked smile. "A polka? That's your go to happy dance?"

I shook my head. "No, I've never danced a polka nor would I know where or how to start one." I pointed to my temple. "This cold has me in a fog, but at least my throat is feeling better."

Briggs pulled his hand out of his pocket. "Then I guess these are too late." He dropped my favorite brand of cherry cough drops on the table. They were the kind that were more sugar and honey than medicine, so they didn't leave a yucky taste in your throat. They were, of course, rather useless in terms of relieving an irritated throat, but sucking on them always reminded me of staying home from school with a cold, camped out on the family room couch with my books, my stuffed animals and my mom's continuous stream of chicken soup and honeyed tea. The cherry cough drops were all part of the deal.

I picked up the box. "Only the greatest boyfriend in the world would search high and low, through deserts and mountains, to find my favorite cherry cough drops."

He leaned back with a satisfied grin. "Once again, I've earned a world title that I'm not entirely sure I deserve. Especially since I crossed no deserts and climbed no mountains. They were sitting right on the shelf at the Danby Drug Store. Right between that smelly stuff my mom used to rub on my chest to quiet my cough and the nasal spray."

"Yes but you remembered that these were my favorite. I think you can still keep the world title." I unwrapped one but then wrapped it back up in its tiny wax paper square. "Guess I'll wait until after the soup, otherwise the minestrone is going to taste like cherry."

"Wise decision. Cough drops are to minestrone as toothpaste is to orange juice," he said.

We were still having a chuckle about his analogy when Franki arrived at the table. "If it isn't my favorite Port Danby couple." She pulled the pencil from behind her ear. "What can I get you two?" as she spoke, her eyes swept toward me. She lowered the order pad and gave me a worried mom look. "You looked flushed and pale. What's wrong?"

I stared up at her in awe. "Wow, you've got that mom instinct down to an art. I suppose raising four kids does make you somewhat of a pro. I'm fine. Just a little head cold. And is it possible to look flushed and pale? Seems like one would cancel out the other."

Franki looked at Briggs for confirmation on her assessment.

He nodded. "Franki's right. It's a little of both."

She lifted her order pad. "You're having some of my chicken noodle soup. No arguments. When the kids are sick, I make a big pot and they're good as new in no time. What are you having, James?" She'd moved on, so I supposed there really was no chance to argue. My appetite for anything but a cherry cough drop, hot tea and my cozy bed was slowly waning anyhow.

I rested back against the cushion and realized it felt incredibly good to relax after the busy morning. Briggs ordered a pastrami sandwich, and Franki hurried off to get the soup.

"Are you ready for your second surprise?" he asked.

I sat forward. "I forgot you mentioned two surprises." I closed my eyes to wait for it.

"Why are you closing your eyes?"

I opened them. "I thought you might place it on the table or something. Is it big? Is it outside?" I peered through the window. "Are we going to have matching motorcycles? I would love to have an excuse to buy a black leather jacket."

His brow rose higher with each of my ridiculous statements. I sat back and fluttered my eyelashes at him coyly. "You'll have to excuse my absurdity. I'm not myself today. What is the surprise?"

"It doesn't come in a box," he said.

"Thank goodness I didn't hold out my left hand when I closed my eyes. That would have been awkward." A clumsy silence ensued. "All right, I'm blaming that last thought on the cold too. Ignore everything I say at this lunch." Briggs and I had lightly discussed an eventual engagement, but it never went beyond that. If I was honest with myself, I wasn't entirely sure I was ready for it yet. I was very much enjoying my independence and my success. Although, I would have been lying if the thought of marrying Detective James Briggs hadn't crossed my mind now and then.

He smiled inwardly . . . to himself and stopped to take a drink of his cola. "As I mentioned, I have a surprise. I was talking to a friend of mine who works at the records office at the city hall building in Mayfield. That particular office has birth and death certificates for people in Mayfield, Port Danby and Chesterton. The records date all the way back to the early 1800s."

I sat forward so quickly I nearly slipped off the smooth vinyl seat. "Did you find something out about the unmarked grave in the Hawksworth family plot?" I had been researching the Hawksworth murders for over two years and had uncovered details but not enough to connect dots or solve the mystery. I was certain the small, unmarked grave had something to do with the tragedy.

"I didn't find out directly about the grave, but I did find Jane Price's death certificate. My friend made me a copy." He pulled a paper out of his pocket.

"You're the most—"

"Wonderful boyfriend in the world," he finished for me. "Or so I've been told."

I unfolded the paper and pulled my glasses from my purse. "It says she died on February 10th, 1906. Doctor Vernon of Seattle, Washington confirmed the death at the Ladies' Auxiliary Health Center." I looked up at Briggs. "It says she died in childbirth. My hunch about the picture Marty showed me was correct. Jane Price was pregnant when she left Port Danby."

"Considering the Victorian values still lingering at the beginning of the twentieth century, I'd say she left Port Danby because she was pregnant," Briggs added.

"And with her father, Harvard Price, being mayor, the scandal would have made all the papers. Politically, it would have been devastating. Although, I must say, the Price family does seem to be invincible in elections. I still can't believe one family has held the mayor's seat all these years."

Franki delivered my soup with a plate full of soda crackers. (They were essential with chicken noodle soup.) "I made sure to scoop up a lot of the carrots and turnips. Some people think it's the chicken and the chicken broth that provide the healing qualities. I think it's all the good chunks of vegetables. Either way, don't leave a drop behind, and I promise you'll feel better by tomorrow."

"Yes, Dr. Franki," I said with a wink.

I scooped up a carrot chunk and stared at it.

"What's wrong? Too hot?" Briggs asked.

"No, this cold just doesn't make anything sound good." I snuck a peek toward the diner counter where Franki was talking with a customer. "You might have to eat some of this soup," I whispered. "Otherwise, I'm going to disappoint Dr. Franki. But eat some first before I contaminate it with all my *germiness*." Franki walked into kitchen. "The coast is clear." I pushed the bowl across to him, spilling a few spoonfuls as it stuttered across the table top.

"It's boiling hot," Briggs whispered loudly back. "Do you expect me to just slurp it up?"

I batted my lashes at him. "The best boyfriend in the world would suffer a scorched tongue to help his lady."

"I'm regretting that title. And after I gave you two surprises." He leaned over and slurped up some good spoonfuls.

"She's coming back this way." I grabbed the bowl away from him with the spoon halfway to his mouth. "Spoon, spoon," I pointed to the utensil. He nearly tossed it into the bowl. More soup spilled. I wiped it up just before Franki reached the table.

Franki smiled down at the slightly emptied bowl. "How is it? I'll bet you're feeling better already."

I lifted the spoon with a big grin. "So good. And yep, I'm feeling like a million bucks. Thanks."

Franki walked away.

"And thank you, my brave boyfriend," I said quietly.

"You can add all the accolades and flattering descriptors you want to the word *boyfriend*, I'm not eating any more chicken soup. And Franki's right. You should have some. It's one of the few home remedies that has withstood the test of time. It's probably completely bogus, but people still swear by it."

I reluctantly took a sip, then decided the warmth of the broth was more comforting than expected.

I patted the copy of the death certificate. "If Jane died in childbirth, what happened to the baby? I wonder if it died too."

Briggs swallowed a bite of sandwich and motioned to the paper. "You didn't get to the small notation at the bottom of the certificate. It's hard to read because the original was faded, but the doctor mentions the baby."

I smoothed the paper out and moved it under the pendant light on the table. "Baby Price, a girl, was sent to live with her father's family in Port Danby. She is lacking in health and vigor and not expected to reach her first birthday."

My face popped up. Briggs was fully absorbed in his lunch. "Port Danby. That unmarked grave in the Hawksworth family plot, I think it's Jane's baby. Which means Bertram Hawksworth was the father. I have no solid proof of that yet, but I think it's a good theory. What do you think, Detective Briggs?"

He wiped his mouth. "I think you're a darn good investigator, Miss Pinkerton. Now eat your chicken soup, or Franki is not going to let us leave this diner."

CHAPTER 4

*R*yder walked in from his lunch break and stopped in the center of the store. "You need to go home and rest. You look like a patch of wilted weeds, and I mean that in the nicest way."

"I'm not feeling too bad despite the resemblance to wilted weeds." I rested the broom against the wall. I'd only been sweeping the floor for a few minutes, but it felt as if I had run an uphill marathon. "I'm determined to go to opening night. I think all I need is some medicine. I'm going to stop by the drug store for some aspirin and cold medicine. I've tried Franki's chicken soup, but now it's time to pull out the big guns, namely the pharmaceuticals. My head seems to be filled with helium gas today. I'm surprised I'm not floating up by the ceiling. Aspirin will clear it right up." As I rambled on about helium and aspirin, I pulled on my coat and buttoned it up good. "Don't let Kingston out anymore today. Even if he paces in front of the door and taps the glass with his beak. I just know he'll head down to the town square and bother the theater group."

"I'll make sure he stays inside." Ryder pulled on a work apron.

"I'm going to put some thyme in pots. Tom said he would set up a special table in Corner Market for our potted herbs. They are getting so popular, they're going to have their own spot in the window."

"That's great. Maybe we'll have to switch the name of the store to Pink's Herbs." I waved. "I'm babbling nonsense again. Goodbye." I stopped and pointed a motherly finger at Kingston. "I'll be right back. Behave and easy on the treats. Your belly is too round. Pretty soon your wings will be as useless as a penguin's wings." With that silly warning, I walked out into the brisk afternoon air.

Most of the people strolling along Harbor Lane had removed their coats and hats. Some had even reduced their outerwear to thin sweaters, but I hunkered down in my winter coat as if a glacial wind was swirling through town.

I was sure a couple of aspirin and some decongestant would do the trick. I didn't want to miss the play. Something told me it was going to be a memorable night.

There was a flurry of activity in the Danby Drug Store. It seemed I was not the only person who was unlucky enough to catch the mid-spring virus. A spinning rack containing every type of cold medicine sat prominently in the center of the store, obviously moved there from its usual location at the back. People were hovering around the spinning rack pulling boxes free to read labels and find just the right medicine for their symptoms. I sidled my way in between a man who was wearing a face mask and a woman whose nose was as red as a tomato and who looked the way I felt, like a patch of wilted weeds. Elbows jammed this way and that and tissues were being dragged from purses and pockets. The unmistakable scent of menthol threatened to overwhelm me, just as it had when I was eight and my mom insisted the odor wouldn't be too bad and that it would help my cough. She'd sorely underestimated my sense of smell and the strength of the menthol fragrance. She had to rush me into the shower where I spent a good ten minutes getting the greasy stuff off my skin, all while trying to hold my nose.

Two more snifflers joined the crowd huddled around the cold medicine. I could almost feel the cloud of germs settling over the spinning display rack. The amount of choices was a little too over-whelming, so I decided to skip the cold medicine and opt for good old fashioned aspirin.

I freed myself from the pushy elbows, runny noses and fevered expressions and headed down the pain reliever aisle. I was steeped in self-pity when I spotted Constance, the actress who had visited the flower shop in the morning. Gordon, the straw blond scarecrow was nowhere in sight. Constance was standing in front of the ointments staring blankly at the various creams.

"Good thinking," I said cheerily.

She glanced my direction. Her eyes and nose were red and puffy, but I was sure it wasn't from a cold. It seemed she'd been crying. She didn't seem to recognize me. Her brows bunched almost as if she was angry. "Excuse me?" she said sharply.

"I'm Lacey, the owner of Pink's Flowers. You came into my shop this morning. How are the red roses?" I decided to skip over her unfriendly demeanor.

"That's right. The roses are fine. Very pretty." She couldn't have been less enthusiastic about the flowers she'd wanted so badly just hours before.

"I guess that rash is still bothering you," I said. "When do you have to get dressed for rehearsal? Hopefully the salve will bring you some relief first."

Her mood was dark, but she seemed somewhat pleased to have someone inquire about her woes.

"The director is having me just play a Munchkin so I can avoid the heavy monkey makeup. It's only a small part," she said, adding in a dejected frown.

"At least you'll have time to recuperate from the rash," I suggested.

"Only to have the rash fire back up when I return to the flying monkey part." Her expression hardened. "They are both silly bit parts."

"When is the dress rehearsal?" I asked brightly, hoping to erase the glower I caused by bringing up the rash.

"Soon." She pulled out her phone. I suspected she was hoping for a text or call rather than checking the time. Her subsequent disappointment indicated there was no text or call. I could only assume she was hoping to hear from Gordon but then I could have been totally off base. After all, my mind wasn't exactly clear and concise, which reminded me that I needed aspirin. Still, I found Constance's utterly changed demeanor interesting. Was it possible she was still upset that Gordon only bought her half a dozen roses?

"I guess Mr. Scarecrow is busy getting his straw nipped and tucked and whatever else they do to transform a human into a straw man." I tapped my chin. "Is the correct reference Mr. Scarecrow or just Scarecrow?"

After perusing the shelves as if she was purchasing her first home, Constance blindly reached for a box of ointment. "If you'll excuse me, I don't want to be late for rehearsal."

I bowed my head. "Of course. Sorry to keep you."

She swooshed past me fast enough to cause a curl on my forehead to flutter. But rushed as she was, she took the time to stop at the end of the aisle and check her phone. I scooted along the shelves past the antacid and foot powder to the aspirin. I grabbed a box and headed toward checkout.

Constance was on the phone. She turned her head away and spoke harshly but quietly into the phone. "Call me back. We need to talk before rehearsal. It's very important." She hung up. Even though I offered her a polite smile, she rushed past me as if we were complete strangers. Which, technically, we were. It seemed there was going to be at least one extra grumpy Munchkin on the stage tonight. Maybe the rash had finally gotten so irritating it put her in a sour mood. Seemed like a perfectly legitimate reason to be grumpy.

Constance paid for the ointment and rushed from the store. I stopped by the small freezer near the checkout counter and pulled out an orange popsicle. We were still a few months shy of popsicle weather, but it sounded refreshing and soothing for my throat. I paid for both items and opened the popsicle wrapper on the way out the door.

My phone rang and I pulled it from my coat pocket with my free hand. I laughed briefly at the notion of enjoying an ice pop while swaddled in a thick winter coat.

"Hello," I said before pushing the pop into my mouth.

"Did Franki's chicken soup do the trick?" Briggs asked.

I licked my lips. "No, I've resorted to more scientific means. I bought some aspirin and a popsicle."

His deep chuckle rumbled through the phone. "Ah ha, so you've been researching the famous scientific study on popsicles and their effects on the common cold."

I pulled the pop from my lips, sound effect and all. "No kidding? Is there really such a study?"

"Wow, kiddo, maybe we should cancel tonight."

My cheeks warmed. "Well, you said it so seriously, and with my head being particularly light, it all sounded quite plausible. It sure would make every kid in the world happy to know that sucking on popsicles could cure their colds. And we're not canceling. I'll be fine. I was just talking to a grumpy Munchkin, which makes me even more eager to see the play."

"Did you say a grumpy Munchkin? I thought Munchkin's were happy members of the Lollipop Guild and all that."

"This particular Munchkin moonlights as a flying monkey, so I guess you could say she has multiple personalities. This morning she came to my shop cheery and begging her boyfriend, the Scarecrow, for roses. She got the roses, but her mood is much darker this afternoon. By the way, is it Mr. Scarecrow or the Scarecrow or just Scarecrow?"

There was a long pause. "Finish the popsicle and take the aspirin. And I can always get tickets for another night if you're not feeling up to it this evening."

"I'll be fine. I can feel the popsicle regimen working already. Maybe there *should* be a scientific study."

"Goodbye, Lacey."

"Goodbye."

CHAPTER 5

*I*t was official. As comforting as a bowl of Franki's chicken soup was, its healing properties didn't hold a candle (or a noodle) to aspirin. Fifteen minutes after taking two aspirin, my chills and body aches vanished and my head cleared, at least as much as was possible. I could only blame the cold for so much of my occasional silliness. I could still vaguely remember pestering Constance in the drug store when she clearly didn't want to be bothered. That was a combination of my feeling out of sorts and my insatiable curiosity. Her change in temperament from morning until afternoon was just so odd, I couldn't help myself. She certainly raced away from me the second she had the chance. I probably deserved it.

"How can I help you?" I asked as my face popped up from behind a vase of mixed spring flowers. "Oh, it's you, Elsie."

"Not exactly a rousing greeting. Especially when I come bearing edible gifts." Elsie marched with her usual energy to the counter. She was holding a plate.

"I'm smelling banana"—I sniffed the air—"cinnamon and walnuts."

She placed the plate of warm muffins on the counter. "You can actually smell walnuts?"

"Not really. But I saw muffins and I smelled banana so I assumed walnut." I reached under the sheet of plastic wrap. "I have to eat one now since they are warm and beckoning me to enjoy them."

Elsie rested her forearm along the edge of the counter. "I heard you were sick." It was rare to see the woman without at least one smudge of flour on her face. Today she had a jagged streak on her forehead that reminded me of Harry Potter. Each day, more and more silver gray replaced the natural caramel color of her hair, but she never looked older. Her stringent routine of running, working hard and never overindulging in her own sweets kept her as fit as an Olympic athlete.

I savored a warm bite of muffin and got a nice surprise. "Ooh, mini chocolate chips too?"

"Surprised you didn't smell the chocolate." Elsie hopped up on a stool.

"I think it's my cold. My olfactory cells are in a fog. How did you know I was sick? And it's just a head cold. You know nothing keeps this old gal down."

"Just keep on your side of the counter, old gal." Elsie waved her fingers to motion me back. "You can still sell flowers with a cold. I cannot bake cookies and cakes. And since I have yet to find a suitable replacement for my niece, Britney, I have no choice except to bake. Otherwise, I'd have to shut down."

"First of all, you are once again holding way too high of a standard for your assistant. What about that last guy, Ted?" I asked.

"Tad. Who names their kid Tad?"

"I'm sure it was short for something. Anyhow, I thought he was pretty good. Fast, efficient and he made a very good pan of brownies. Not as good as yours," I added quickly. "But they were tasty."

"Yes, well he was slow at frosting cakes."

I stared at her. "That was it? He couldn't frost cakes fast enough?"

Elsie shrugged. "Among other things." Somehow without looking, she sensed she had flour on her forehead. She used the back of her hand to wipe it off, then tapped the counter. "I came in here to tell you something funny. So I'm placing cookies on a silver tray and the door opens and the Scarecrow and Dorothy walk inside and order two lemon tarts. The actors were in full costume. The Scarecrow even left a few pieces of straw on my floor. Dorothy was pretty but a little taller than I would have expected and her eyes were sort of small. Not like Judy Garland's eyes at all. Now those were a pair of eyes." She laughed. "I thought it was funny because when I watched the movie as an adult, I always wondered if, you know, any hanky panky ever happened between Dorothy and one of her traveling companions. Of course, I always thought it would be the Tin Man. He was taller and a little more masculine than the other two."

I stared unblinkingly at her as she finished her long moment of bizarre contemplation. I wasn't exactly sure how to respond.

She looked at me. "Isn't it funny? I mean they were definitely flirting. Well, as much as the guy covered in straw and makeup could flirt. He offered her his tattered old coat on the way out because she was wearing that little puffed sleeve gingham dress."

"I'm still trying to process the notion of you imagining a romantic link between Dorothy and her three companions. I don't think I've ever once considered that there could be—Wait, did you say the Scarecrow and Dorothy? But the Scarecrow has been dating one of the Munchkins for two years. He bought her six red roses this morning."

Elsie squinted in thought. "Wasn't it Tin Man who was in love with a Munchkin and that was why he was looking for his heart?"

I laughed. "If someone walked in here right now and heard two perfectly normal grown women debating the romantic threads in *The Wizard of Oz*, they would walk right back out and never return. But back to what you saw. You're sure it was the Scarecrow and Dorothy?"

She arched a brow. "Really?"

I nodded. "Of course. How could you confuse either of those characters? Was the Scarecrow tall with blue eyes?"

"I didn't take too close of a look at his eyes, but he was tall with nice shoulders. And Dorothy had shiny auburn hair. Like I said, she was pretty and apparently quite smitten with her straw man."

"Well, this explains why Constance was in such a frazzled state," I said to myself.

"Who is Constance?" Elsie asked.

"A Munchkin and she also plays the part of a flying monkey. The makeup gave her a rash, but I think there was more to her irritation than itchy red patches."

Elsie hopped off the stool. "Well, this whole conversation is starting to sound like gibberish, and I have two apple pies in the oven. Enjoy the muffins and feel better."

"Thanks." I sat down on a stool to finish my snack. Kingston flew over to join me. I broke off a crumb, and he plucked it from my fingertips. "Well, well, King. Looks like this play is going to be more entertaining than I expected."

Ryder walked into the shop. "Lola got in a bunch of those post-mortem Victorian pictures. Those things are so creepy, but she thinks they're cool."

I put my hands on my hips. "So an actor in monkey makeup freaks her out, but pictures of dead people dressed and posed as if they were alive and enjoying everyday life are cool. She is a weird person. Escape now while you have your chance."

Naturally, I was joking, but Ryder's face dropped and his earlier smile faded.

"That's it. I knew something was up with you. You haven't been your usual self." I walked closer to him but kept a good, safe distance to avoid passing on my cold.

His shoulders lifted with a deep breath. "I've been asked to join a team of researchers in Brazil. They are studying medicinal plants in the Amazon. It's a three month expedition, and it would be great experience."

I threw my arms up and was about to hug him but stopped short. "Man, I really hate this cold." I threw my arms out and hugged an invisible person. "There, one of my special long distance hugs. But I don't understand—why are you so sad? This seems perfect for you."

He raked his long bangs back off his face. "It is. But I'd be leaving you without an assistant right in the middle of bridal season and then there's—" His gaze drifted to the windows.

"Then there's Lola," I finished for him. "So you haven't mentioned this to her yet?"

"No, because I'm a coward. Maybe I need to head to Oz for some courage."

"First of all, don't worry about the flower shop. I'll manage. I'm sure I can find an assistant. And if they work out, they can stay. Business has been good, and I think we both could use a hand during busy seasons." I walked back to the mixed spring bouquets I'd been working on when Elsie walked in. "Ryder, I'm sure Lola will be happy for you. She'll be sad and upset. I don't think I'd be terribly happy if James told me he was leaving the country for three months, but if it was for a good reason, I'd understand. Lola will too."

He raked his fingers through his hair again, assuring me that telling Lola was making him anxious. "They've given me a week to decide, so I have some time to think about it. Let's switch subjects. This one gives me a stomachache. You haven't mentioned the

Hawksworth murders for awhile. Are you still working on the case?"

I nearly pushed over the vase I was filling. "Oh my gosh, yes. Thanks to James, I had a big breakthrough today. Remember I told you that I thought Jane Price, Mayor Price's great aunt, had some kind of connection to all of it?"

"Yeah, you said Marty found an old picture of Jane Price. She was sent out of town or something." Ryder started placing newly potted herbs in our delivery wagon.

"Right. I'm pretty sure I know why. She was pregnant and unmarried. A scandal like that would have hurt the Price family name, so it makes sense that Harvard Price, her father, sent her away. Sadly, it turns out she died in childbirth. The baby girl was sickly. She was sent back to Port Danby to live with her father."

Ryder looked up from his task. "But you said she was unmarried." He blushed. "Of course, there still has to be a father. Learned that in biology," he chuckled.

"Right. I think Bertram Hawksworth was the baby's father." I leaned back to admire the arrangement.

"Wow, double scandal right here in little ole Port Danby. Do you know for certain?"

"No, darn it," I said. "I need to find out what happened to the baby. She wasn't expected to live long, poor thing."

Ryder put the last pot in the wagon, then snapped his fingers. "Hey, did you know there's an entire file of Port Danby obituaries stored in the mayor's office? They date back to the mid 1800s. I know because I had to do a local history report on Dick Duggin. He was the town's first doctor. His obituary was in the file. The guy was a doctor, but he didn't take too good care of himself. He died from a heart attack. You should check it out. You might find an obituary for the baby."

"That is a brilliant idea. I've been meaning to take a stroll through the town square to check out the activities. I can drop the herbs off on my way and pick up the wagon from Tom on the trip back."

"Guess you're feeling better then?" he said.

"Yes, I am. I think a walk will do me good."

CHAPTER 6

I'd been so sheltered in my head cold and feeling out of it, I hadn't had a chance to walk to the town square to witness the extravagant chaos that went along with setting up for a large theater production. I could feel the energy in the misty sea air as I walked out of Corner Market and turned onto Pickford Way. Marty's lovely lady, the Pickford Lighthouse, glistened in the late afternoon sun. The earlier chill still clung to the air, but cold temperatures were always much more tolerable when the sun was shining. Two aspirin had made it more tolerable as well. The shivers and aches that had kept me under the weather all morning were gone. (I hoped for good but I wasn't counting on it.)

The massive tent erected for the play was nearly blinding in whiteness. It billowed and collapsed lightly as the usual afternoon breeze wafted up from the beach below. The winter weary branches of the ironwood trees surrounding the town square were bursting with tender green leaves, whispering promises of a lush, cooling summer shade. True signs of spring had come late this year, and aside from the towering evergreens on the edges of town, the local trees were working hard to catch up to get ready for their showy summer debuts.

The theater group had arrived in a train of large trucks and small trailers. It was quite the production. I could only imagine the logistics of carrying everything from venue to venue. But it was also easy to see why a group would take on the Herculean task of traveling to location. This way they could reach a much wider audience and gain recognition across the country. The Auburn Theater Group had received high praise from critics everywhere, and Mayor Price was particularly proud to book them for our town.

Two flying monkeys (sans wings) scurried past me holding cups of Les's coffee and chatting about an after party. Their makeup and costumes were quite impressive. I could almost see why Lola was a little freaked out.

A crew of three stagehands wheeled a beautifully painted house facade into the tent. It looked just like Aunt Em's quaint farmhouse. Fake trees were rolled in behind it. A loud sound check echoed inside the tent where someone was reciting the obligatory 'testing one two three' chant. It was going to be a great play, and I was looking forward to a night out with Briggs.

Pedestrians were blocked from walking through the activity, so I took the sidewalk that ran behind the town square. With each step closer to the mayor's office, my apprehension grew. Mayor Price had taken an instant disliking to me and my unusual pet from the start, and the two of us never formed a friendship. In fact, I'd only added salt to the wound by making the mistake of asking him about his Great Aunt Jane. He grew red faced and flustered and made it clear he didn't want me nosing around in his family history. With any luck, his receptionist, Ms. Simpson, would be able to point me to the obituary files, and I wouldn't have to deal with Mayor Price at all.

My wish for luck worked. Mayor Price, with his oversized belly and overstretched polyester suit, was standing in the middle of the activity talking to several of the theater hands. He was certainly engaged in this event. I was going to take it as my cue to snoop around in the city records. I picked up my pace.

As I rounded the corner where the dressing trailers had been parked, loud, angry voices shot toward me. Two women seemed to be having an argument. I peered casually between the trailers, trying not to look nosy and, at the same time, being nosy. (One helped negate the other, in my opinion.)

A tall woman with auburn hair tied in two pigtails and wearing the iconic blue and white checked Dorothy of Oz dress was looming over a short, squat woman with a blue cap that had the word Director emblazoned across the front. Gordon and Constance had mentioned her name was Susana. I didn't know much about show business, but I always pictured the director as being the boss, the commander in chief, as it were. But while Susana's voice was what one would expect for the position, loud and booming, she seemed to be shrinking from Dorothy's scolding. I would have crossed the line on nosiness (if there was one) if I'd gone close enough to hear the exact details of their fight, but there was no doubt that they were in the middle of a rambunctious disagreement. Every time Susana attempted to show her authority by stretching taller and talking louder, her opponent, Dorothy, would get angrier and lean closer, causing Susana to shrink back. It was all somewhat amusing and ironic considering the angry woman was wearing a sweet checked pinafore and ribbon tied pigtails. Still, costume or not, she was intimidating, and the director was getting a tongue lashing she wouldn't soon forget. The few spare words I was able to catch clearly were about a dressing table mirror and having to put up with a clumsy makeup artist. It seemed Dorothy really considered herself quite the irreplaceable star.

I was just about to pull myself away from the scene when my

gaze drifted past a familiar face. Naturally, a few of the cast members had gathered just past the trailers to watch the spectacle. Constance's face was amongst the crowd, and there was no denying that she was wearing an amused grin. It looked just right with her rosy red Munchkin cheeks, fake yellow hair and brightly colored costume with glittery collars and cuffs. As was to be expected, in a group that traveled together, there seemed to be a lot of dynamics and small soap opera style subplots between the members. It probably made for some great drama on the road, but at the same time, it would be stressful. I loved Lola and Elsie and Les, but our friendships would be strained if we had to spend a significant amount of time traveling together from town to town.

It was time to stop dawdling. I had a short window of opportunity to do some research, and I needed to hurry along.

CHAPTER 7

Mayor Price was still out and about meandering through the activity with that self-important grin he had perfected. I picked up the pace and headed to the small brick house with the white trim and columns, a far too cozy and congenial looking building for the perpetually grumpy mayor.

Lanky, long faced Ms. Simpson, Mayor Price's fastidious and efficient assistant, hunched over her desk as she finished writing something with a pen. She heard the door open but didn't look up from her task. "I'll be right with you." She reached across her desk, picked up a stamp, pressed it on an ink pad and smacked the stamp down hard on the paper in front of her. She took her time placing the stamp back down, folding the paper in three and adding a staple to the whole thing. Then she looked up and dropped her chin to peer over the top of her gold framed glasses.

"May I help you?" she asked in a tone that didn't fit the polite inquiry.

"Hi, I'm Lacey Pinkerton. I own Pink's Flowers," I continued, even though she knew exactly who I was.

"Yes. Nice to see you." Again, the tone didn't quite match the kind sentiment.

"Nice to see you too." (My tone matched the words, but it wasn't entirely sincere.) The truth was, I'd had several interactions with Ms. Simpson, and none of them had been positive. It was as if her boss, Mayor Price, had warned her ahead of time to be rude and indifferent to the town florist. I just wasn't sure how I'd earned such a distinction.

I stood politely holding my hands in front of me like a kid about to ask the teacher for permission to erase the chalkboard. "I'm hoping you can help me, Ms. Simpson." I decided it was always a nice added touch to address someone by their formal name. It seemed to soften her a bit. "I was told that this office had a file of town obituaries."

Her long nose scrunched back enough to send her glasses to the tip. She pushed them back. "Yes, there is a file of obituaries. We don't usually get people asking to see it. Occasionally, a grade school student comes in to research a local historical figure. I'll assume you're not writing a social studies report." Obviously amused by her comment, her lips straightened in a suppressed smile.

I decided to play along. Humor, no matter how wry and biting, always helped melt ice. And there were definitely a few glaciers in my path. "Yes, my desert habitat and Native American reports are behind me, thank goodness. I'm researching a death from the year 1906." I decided long before I'd made the journey to the mayor's office that I wouldn't bring up the Hawksworth name. "I assume the files are in some kind of chronological order."

My question threw her off the path of inquisition she seemed headed down. She adjusted her shiny gold glasses again. "Yes, of course. Organization is the key to running a tight ship."

I nodded. "I said that to myself the first time we met. I said that Ms. Simpson runs a tight ship. I mean, just look at this place." I waved my arms around the impeccably neat office. My overtures worked.

Ms. Simpson rose from her chair and pulled a set of keys from the top desk drawer. "Obviously, you can't take the files out of this office, and I can't have you sitting in the center of the room doing research."

"Obviously," I concurred, although there just wasn't that much foot traffic going in and out of the mayor's office that I'd get in the way.

She walked over and opened a set of folding closet doors revealing a wall of metal file cabinets, each one labeled. Her long legs folded as she stooped down to a bottom file in the right corner of the closet. She unlocked the drawer and rolled it open. I moved my head side to side to get a look outside the front window. Most of the activity in the town square was blocked by the line of parked trailers, but I couldn't see anyone, and by anyone I meant Mayor Price, walking toward the mayor's office.

"This file is dated from 1904 to 1908." Ms. Simpson's voice pulled my attention from the window. She was standing in front of me with a manila folder in her long fingers. She glanced out the window, then back toward me. "I suggest you hurry. Mayor Price doesn't like people loitering around the office with no real purpose." (It seemed our brief friendship was over.)

I took hold of the file. "I'll be quick."

"You can use the desk in that small alcove across the room. The light switch is on the right. Make sure the files go back exactly as you found them, in chronological order."

"Yes, of course." I took the folder across the room. The small alcove held a walnut desk and matching chair. A green canister with pens and pencils and a notepad sat at the top edge of the desk.

I pulled out the chair and sat down with the folder. It was hard to know whether a town would take the time to write an obituary for a young baby, but it was my best chance of finding out what happened to Jane Price's daughter.

After thumbing through the first obituaries, I saw a pattern and came to a conclusion. The year 1905 ended with a terrible flu season that took many people unexpectedly, including the local school teacher and Roland Everton, the man who'd run the local tailor shop for twenty years. I thumbed through the first few months of 1906. Jane's death certificate had noted that she died on February 10th, and the baby was sent to Port Danby after that. So I skipped over to mid-February and flipped through each page. There were far too many young deaths, children in their teens and women and men younger than me, but it was a common occurrence back then. How hard it must have been in those days to endure so many losses. And losing a child, while I wasn't a mother, I could only imagine. As my mom once put it, losing a child would be like having your breath stolen from you every morning as you rose from bed, painful and nearly impossible to survive.

I shook the bleak thoughts from my head. Apparently, obituary hunting wasn't as uplifting as one might think. I reached the end of March 1906 and a gasp caught in my throat. All these months of research and it finally felt as if I was getting close to solving everything. The small, yellowed obituary had been cut from a newspaper using somewhat dull scissors. Two of the corners had disappeared with age, but the text was still complete and only slightly faded. The obituary writer started with the words, *Another tiny angel has left us. It is with sadness that I report the tragic and untimely death of Jennifer P. H. Her mother was lost in childbirth, and her little angel followed shortly after. Mother and daughter are rejoined for eternity. May they be forever at peace.*

I stared down at the brittle piece of newspaper. "Jennifer P. H. The baby's names were Price Hawksworth," I muttered.

"What are you up to now!" Mayor Price barked over my shoulder.

CHAPTER 8

he mayor's sharp tone startled me so much, I sat back hard. The chair rocked, tipped back on two legs, then slammed back to four. I twisted around. Mayor Price's angry, red face hovered over me. His arms were crossed tightly over his belly, and he glowered down at me with wide, twitching nostrils.

I caught my breath, although it was going to take several minutes for my pulse to slow. I swallowed and calmly put the obituary back into its proper place. After all, I wasn't doing anything wrong or illegal. I was merely rummaging through public records.

I took another steadying breath before pushing to my feet. Mayor Price's wide girth filled the small alcove leaving me little room to maneuver away from the desk. I glanced toward the front office hoping Ms. Simpson would gain a bit of compassion or an ounce of humanness and come to my rescue, but she pretended to busy herself with work on her desk. It was easy to see that she had a full ear tilted our direction so as not to miss one word of my subsequent scolding. Only I wasn't about to take this like some kid getting caught for staying out after curfew. I was a grown woman, and I wasn't doing anything wrong.

I lifted my chin and held the manila folder tightly in my hand. "Mayor Price, nice to see you," I said with forced cheer (and a slight waver). I held up the folder. "As you see, I was perusing some of the public records for this marvelous town. I'm always interested in the history of Port Danby, so I decided to sift through the obituaries from the early twentieth century. Very interesting stuff, by the way." I was just nervous enough to ramble on. "Did you know a terrible strain of influenza killed dozens of people at the end of 1905?" I forced a soft chuckle. "Of course, you know that. You're the mayor and a member of a prominent family. Well, I'm all through here so I won't keep you."

His stoney expression hadn't softened one bit and he hadn't budged an inch. I was stuck in the alcove with the mayor's thick form acting as a fourth wall. "I heard you say the Price name. You're snooping into my family history again. How many times do I need to tell you to stay out of my business." A bit of spittle shot from his rubbery lips. There was little space for me to dodge safely out of its trajectory but I managed.

It was time to drop the polite charade. "Not that it's really any of *your* business, but I'm researching the Hawksworth family murder. It has nothing to do with your family." I included the last piece hoping I would get a reaction of some sort, but he was so angry the only things moving on his face were his twitchy nostrils.

Then, without warning, a hard laugh shot from his mouth. "You're wasting your time. That case was solved by the police the week after it happened. Bertram Hawksworth was in financial distress, so he killed his family and committed suicide. Why don't you stick to selling flowers." His suggestion came with a simpering grin that made his round cheeks rise up and swallow his deep set eyes.

His unearned wrath and what I perceived as a dramatic overreaction on his part, emboldened me. "Well, I believe the Port Danby Police were wrong. In fact, the first officer to investigate the

tragedy wrote his misgivings in his report but then he was myste-
riously sent to another precinct before he could follow up."

The mayor's face was red nearly up to the forehead and he was
huffing. "You're just creating a mystery out of nothing. Why don't
you find something better to occupy your time."

I smiled. "Yes, like selling flowers. I'd rather investigate the
Hawksworth murders, and since there is no ordinance against it," I
added for a stinging barb. During my first six months in Port
Danby, Mayor Price tried to persuade the city council to pass an
ordinance banning crows from businesses and shops. By then,
Kingston had won over so many fans, the ordinance was voted
down by the council. It was a solid and aggravating defeat for the
mayor, and it made him dislike me even more. (Not that I needed
help with that.)

I, rather rudely, waved my fingers at him, letting him know he
should move. He turned to the side. I had to sidle around his belly.
He really had no right to berate me. I decided to toss out a little
nugget to assure him my investigation wasn't frivolous. It would
also help me solidify my theory about the unmarked Hawksworth
grave.

"By the way, I found the obituary for your Great Aunt Jane's
baby." He stared at me with a wild-eyed look that nearly made me
stop my comments. (Nearly.) "What a tragedy that the baby only
lived a month. At least Bertram Hawksworth made sure she had a
proper burial. Even if no one took the time to mark her grave."

Mayor Price's bulging eyes looked toward Ms. Simpson. She
still pretended to be working, but I was certain she'd heard every
word. His tongue seemed to have twisted up in his mouth because
his lips moved but no words came out. His reaction was all I
needed to confirm my suspicions.

"You are out of control and spreading malicious lies about my
family. I've heard enough." He reached for the folder and yanked it
from my hand. "And keep that crow out of the town square or I'll

have animal control throw a net over him and take him away. Just a few minutes ago, I saw that menacing beast steal off with one of the actor's leftover sandwich."

"Speaking of spreading lies—My bird is sitting on his perch in the shop window. Good day, Mayor Price. I guess I'll see you at opening night. Should be a wonderful play." I added a pleasant smile, nodded toward Ms. Simpson (who was still putting on quite the show of being interminably busy) and headed out the door. My phone was out and dialed before I reached the bottom step.

CHAPTER 9

ey, baby, I was just about to call you. How are you feeling?"

Even though every hair on my body was still at attention and adrenaline still pumped furiously through my veins, the sound of Briggs' deep, soothing tone coupled with him calling me 'baby', an occasional term of endearment that always left me dizzy, soothed my nerves and brought me back to earth.

"I just had the most unpleasant conversation with our mayor." My words were coming in spurts between breaths. "What an aggravating man. He is utterly without charm, decency and—and —Argh, he's so devoid of personality I can't even think of another term."

"Calm down, Lacey. First of all, why were you talking to Mayor Price? You usually avoid him."

"Usually. Only this time, I was inside the mayor's office, so it was hard to avoid him. Although, in my defense, I thought he was still out in the town square. I was sure I could get in and out of the office without seeing him. But my luck abandoned me on that front."

"Why were you in the mayor's office?"

"I was telling Ryder about the information you found on Jane Price. He mentioned that there was a file of obituaries stored in the mayor's office. He used it once to research a social studies project. I went there to find out if there was an obituary for Jane's baby. And there was. But the mayor walked in while I was reading it. Then, I might have said something to myself about the baby being both a Price and a Hawksworth and he overheard."

"I'll bet he didn't take too kindly to that. What did he say?"

I stopped and took a nice, deep breath. "Oh, if I go through it again right now it'll only make me more upset. Hearing your voice is starting to help calm me down, so let's not spoil it. I'll tell you all about it when my hackles are no longer raised. However, I have some interesting details to add to the Hawksworth mystery." I headed back toward Pickford Way and the theater chaos. The disagreeable conversation with Mayor Price had added energy to my step. "I'll tell you this. The Price family had something to do with that murder. I'm sure of it. I think that's why Mayor Price dislikes me so much. I'm snooping into hidden family secrets."

"How about I bring you dinner at your place tonight before the play? You can tell me all about it."

"That sounds perfect. Bring something warm but not too spicy or too filling."

"Any suggestions?" he asked.

"Nope. Surprise me."

His phone beeped to alert him of another call. "That's a call I've been waiting for. So you're still feeling up to a play tonight?"

"Oh yes. Wouldn't miss it. I'll let you go. See you tonight."

"Bye."

As I rounded a corner of one of the trailers, I looked down to push my phone into my coat and ran smack dab into none other than the Tin Man.

"Excuse me," he said. He was a good foot taller than me as I stared up into his silver face. The lingering smell of tobacco suggested that he had just stepped away from the activity to have a smoke. Interestingly enough, the pungent odor of tobacco was mixed with something much more herbal, rosemary according to my never wrong nose.

"No, it was all my fault. I wasn't looking where I was going," I said. "Of course, the last thing I expected was to run into a Tin Man. An experience I won't soon forget." I was just being polite, but he seemed to instantly take it as flirting.

It was more than a touch comical for him to put on a suave expression as he spoke as if he'd forgotten he was coated in silver makeup while wearing a funnel on his head and holding an oil can in his hand. "It was all my *pleasure*. I won't forget it either. Are those curls natural?"

I primped my curls up with a hand. "Naturally annoying, yes. But we're stuck with what nature gives us, eh?" I stepped sideways to let him know I was on my way.

He laughed and moved to meet my sideways step. "Beautiful and funny. Nice combination."

The conversation needed a sharp turn. "Speaking of combinations—do your cigarettes contain rosemary? I'm getting a distinctly Italian food sort of vibe from you."

He laughed again and lifted the oil can. "The prop crew ran out of oil for the can. Apparently, the Corner Market was fresh out of plain old vegetable oil. So they filled my can with rosemary infused olive oil."

"Oh my, the Tin Man is really moving into gourmet territory. Might have to bring some garlic sticks to opening night."

He raised his brows, inadvertently dislodging some of the silver makeup. "Are you coming to opening night?"

"Yes, with my boyfriend," I added pointedly. It was my chance to find out what the earlier hullaballoo was all about. "I have to say —I was worried that the opening night would be delayed."

"Why is that?" he asked.

Right then, one of the crew members poked his head around the corner of the trailer. "Hey, Johnny, if you're through with your smoke break, Susie needs to see you."

"Be right there," he answered, then returned his silver face toward me for a response.

"It's just that when I walked by earlier, the actress playing Dorothy and the woman wearing the director's hat were having a terrible argument." I pointed between the trailers. "They were standing right there, so it was hard to miss."

"Oh that. Nah, that wouldn't affect opening night. Susana, the director and Amanda, the actress who plays Dorothy, rarely see eye to eye on anything. They are constantly fighting. Amanda is spoiled and Susana is spineless."

"Well, James and I have had tickets for a few months, so I'm glad they were able to solve their differences. It just wouldn't be *The Wizard of Oz* with a grumpy Dorothy."

"Whoever James is, I'm thoroughly jealous." It seemed we were back to the awkward, one-sided flirt session. "Amanda will put on a good performance. She never lets anything get in the way of her art, but I doubt they solved their differences. Even if they had, there would just be a new set of differences right behind it. They will never like each other but that's all right. Wouldn't be the first time a director and a leading star didn't get along. I've got to go. If you ever get tired of this guy James, you know where to find me."

"Yes, you'll be the one wearing silver makeup and a funnel hat," I said as he walked off. He seemed properly embarrassed, although I was sure he was the kind of guy who didn't stay embarrassed for long.

I took another deep breath. What an excursion it had been. I needed to get back to the quiet of my shop just to gather my thoughts. It had been quite an afternoon.

CHAPTER 10

e closed the flower shop early. Opening night had caused a quick desertion of town, allowing people to go home, eat dinner and dress for the theater. It was amusing to think of Port Danby shutting down to dress for the theater, as if our little town had been dropped back into another time and place where culture and live dramas and musicals were as commonplace as sitting to a night of television. As much as I didn't agree with anything Mayor Price did or said, I had to hand him this little victory. Booking a theater group for *The Wizard of Oz* was amazing. And I would've been looking extremely forward to it if some of my more annoying symptoms hadn't returned.

I'd gone straight home to a cup of tea and the knitted throw on my couch. Nevermore, with his keen cat sense, knew the second his human stepped in the door she needed her fur covered heating pad. He'd curled up neatly in my lap and purred out his radiant cat heat. Smartly, I'd downed two more aspirin before hibernating under my throw, so I was feeling a good deal better and somewhat drowsy when Briggs' knock startled me to attention and sent my four pawed heating pad off my lap and into the bedroom.

Briggs wore a worried look. His phone was clutched in his hand. "I texted but you didn't answer," he said as he walked inside. The aroma of rosemary and tomato drifted to my nose from the white bag he carried in his other hand.

"Sorry, I was in a mild and pleasant state of warm delirium. My phone must have still been in my coat pocket."

He looked down at the rumpled blanket and the mostly empty tea cup, then turned back to me. He'd pulled on one of his nicest sweaters and his usually unruly hair was neatly combed. (It was appropriate for the night's event, but I never grew tired of his usual uncombed look.) "You're still not feeling well. Lacey, why don't we cancel? We can just stay in tonight."

"Nonsense. We've both been looking forward to this night out. I took some aspirin. It did wonders for me earlier today." I took the bag of food from his hand and carried it to the kitchen. "This smells good. Ravioli from Mama Jean's?"

"And breadsticks," he added. "I know you said nothing too spicy, so I compromised with Italian."

I pulled down two plates. "You did well, sir. An hour ago, I might have cringed, but now I'm in the mood for pasta."

Briggs followed me into the kitchen. "What did our fair mayor have to say exactly?"

I sensed a slight jaw clench, which meant Briggs was not feeling too friendly toward Mayor Price at the moment. I decided not to add any fuel to the potential fire.

I shrugged lightly. "Oh, you know, the usual grumpy comments. He just doesn't like me. Do you know he tried to blame Kingston for stealing someone's sandwich? He thinks every crow is Kingston."

"He's always consistent in his ignorance, I'll give him that." Briggs walked up next to me, instantly swaddling me in his cozy, manly warmth and the scent of his soap. "This afternoon, when you called me, you were very upset. What did he say? I think I need to have a talk with the man."

I spun to him but resisted the urge to kiss him. Darn germs. "I'm a big girl, and I think I handled him just fine. He's upset about me investigating the Hawksworth murders, and that's because his great grandfather, Havard Price, was somehow involved in the tragedy. I think it's one of those dark family secrets he's trying very hard to keep secure."

"I'm sure that has him worried. Just don't get ahead of yourself. You don't want to start rumors or gossip before you have actual evidence."

I blinked at him. "Thank you, Detective Briggs. After all, this is my first murder investigation."

"How do you manage to make sarcasm look so cute?" He pulled me closer and, to be safe, kissed my forehead. "I'm sorry I questioned your methods. You're one of the best investigators I know."

I leaned back. "One of them?"

"O.K. the best. Definitely the most fun to kiss. Except when you have a cold."

"Don't remind me. I can't wait for this quarantine period to be over."

The aroma of garlic, oregano and rosemary filled my small house as we carried our plates to the table. "You mentioned on the phone that you had more details about the Hawksworth case. You were looking at old obituaries?" he asked.

"Yes, a somewhat depressing task but it proved fruitful." I plucked a breadstick from the bag and broke off a piece. "I'm almost a hundred percent sure that Jane Price had Bertram Hawksworth's baby, and the child is buried in the unmarked grave in the Hawksworth family plot."

"*Almost* a hundred percent certain?" he asked.

"You're not going back to that same old lecture, are you?" I asked, somewhat disappointed that he'd focused on that *trite* detail rather than the explosive revelations. "I'm not going to take out a front page in the local paper announcing that the late Mayor Harvard Price was grandfather to Bertram Hawksworth's illegitimate baby. Thought you'd be more interested in the information I found." I sat back and nibbled on my breadstick.

"I am." He shook his head once. "Sorry, I guess I'm still sore about the way Price spoke to you today."

"Forget about it. I've hardly given it a second thought."

Briggs always knew when I was lying. He stared at me as he ate a ravioli waiting for me to confess.

"All right, so I have given it a second thought . . . and maybe a third and a fourth. But now I'm going to wipe it from my mind because I'm looking forward to a wonderful evening at the theater." I added a posh accent for the last part of the sentence because it seemed the right thing to do.

"The theater where we'll no doubt run into Mayor Price," he reminded me.

I lifted my chin and straightened my posture. "I'll ignore him, and I'm sure he'll do the same. Now let's get back to the good stuff."

"I apologize in advance for sprinkling on what you have termed as the stinky cheese." Briggs sprinkled some parmesan on his ravioli. It was a cheese that smelled far too strong for my sensitive nose so I rarely used it.

I lifted the garlic stick to my nose to mask the smell of the parmesan. He caught my little trick and chuckled. "I find it interesting that parmesan is too strong, but garlic never seems to bother you."

"If it's not too heavy, garlic is a pleasant aroma. I can't say the same for the stinky cheese."

He wiped his mouth after a bite. "All right, so what did you find in your obituary research?"

"There was a sweetly written obituary for a baby girl who died in March of 1906, just a month after Jane Price. Her mother died in childbirth and the baby died soon after. All the other obituaries had full names, but for this particular one they called her Jennifer P. H.." I shifted proudly in my chair and nodded once. "Jennifer Price Hawksworth."

"Or Jennifer Patricia Harris," he noted.

My straight posture deflated. "Since when are you so cynical?"

"You're right. I don't know why I'm being so contrary tonight. I guess I just don't want you to get ahead of yourself on this. It all sounds very plausible, and Jane Price's death certificate certainly fits with your theory. But answer me this. Do you think Hawksworth fathering a baby with Harvard Price's daughter was enough for him to murder the entire family? I know babies out of wedlock were definitely frowned upon back then, but it was hardly a scandal worthy of such a horrendous crime."

"That has definitely crossed my mind." I was feeling a little more inflated now that he was earnestly discussing my theory. I sat forward and picked up my fork. "I could see Harvard wanting to kill Bertram for the affair that eventually destroyed his daughter's life and left the potential for a big political scandal, but why take out Mrs. Hawksworth and the children? There must have been more to the story." I stabbed a fat square ravioli with my fork. "Guess there are more rocks to overturn. I'll figure it out. Just wait and see."

"I look forward to your final report, Miss Pinkerton. I'm sure it'll be a doozy."

CHAPTER 11

*B*riggs and I lingered far too long over our dinner. We found ourselves scurrying around to look for car keys and coats so we wouldn't be late for the play.

We rounded the corner of my street. "You know—if you put your light and siren out, then we could blow through the two stop signs between us and the town square." I smiled hopefully at him.

"You know I'm not going to do that," he said.

"Spoilsport," I muttered and sat back. I'd decided to wear my warmest coat and toss a knitted scarf around my neck to keep the chill out. Heaters had been rolled into the massive theater tent, but I wasn't going to take a chance. The aspirin seemed to be doing their magic. With any luck, I'd make it through the entire performance without so much as a shiver or a sneeze.

Most people had been shuttled down to the town square from various central meeting spots, but my house was only a few miles away. It would have been a waste of time for us to drive farther away just to meet up with a shuttle to drive us back through town.

"Those shuttles were a good idea. Parking is limited," Briggs said. "Looks like we'll have to park here on Harbor Lane and walk to the play." He pulled over in front of Lola's Antiques and across from my store. "Are Lola and Ryder coming tonight?" he asked as he parked the car.

"No way. Lola is terrified of the flying monkeys."

A short laugh spurted from his mouth, then he looked at me. "You're being serious."

"I sure am."

"I didn't figure Lola as the type to fear flying monkeys. She seems more like the type of person who would own one as a pet."

I sucked in a shocked breath. "Are you saying she's a wicked witch?"

"What? No. That's not what I meant at all. You know what? Let's go before I push my foot farther into my mouth this evening."

"You do seem to have a propensity for it tonight," I mused as he stepped out of the car.

He whipped around to my side, opened the door and offered me his hand.

"Thank you, kind sir," I said. "You're momentarily forgiven for the many foot in mouth comments this evening."

We passed the police station. Officer Chinmoor was on duty. Briggs was tempted to pop his head inside and check that things were under control, but I reminded him it was his night off so he walked on without stopping in.

The hum of many voices coasted around the corner as we reached Pickford Way. "Looks like we're not late at all. They haven't even let people inside yet." Briggs pulled out his watch to check the time. "Showtime is in ten minutes."

"It seems odd that everyone would still be standing outside the tent." I pushed up my scarf. "And a damp fog is rolling on shore. I was counting on going straight into the warm, dry tent. Guess it's good I dressed for a blizzard." I took hold of his arm and pulled him closer.

"You might be a little overdressed but not if we're stuck out in the cold. They must be behind schedule." We headed toward the large crowd gathered outside the tent. Most were dressed as if we were all attending a major production on Broadway rather than a traveling play under a canvas tent.

"Detective Briggs." A smartly dressed man I'd seen around town but didn't know walked straight over to us with purpose filled steps. The man had graying sideburns and a serious furrow to his brows. "Maybe you can do something about this. We've been waiting out here in the cold fog for an hour, and they still haven't opened the tent. Mayor Price is nowhere to be found. If you ask me, he's probably hiding from this disgruntled crowd. We are getting plenty agitated. My wife, Marianne"—he waved back to several women and another well-dressed man huddled together talking and laughing—"she catches cold easily. She shouldn't have to stand out here and catch her death after we paid a good amount of money to be sitting inside the theater and not outside of it." He finally took a breath. His bright blue bowtie did a little dance on his neck.

"I'm not entirely sure what I can do, but I suppose I could make my way to the front and find one of the crew members. Otherwise, this really doesn't fall under my jurisdiction," Briggs said lightly to try and jolly the man out of his sour disposition. It didn't work.

Briggs took hold of my hand. "Stay close so I don't lose you in this crowd of disgruntled theater goers. They could turn into an angry, fashionably dressed mob at any minute," he joked, although from the tense energy bouncing around the group he might not have been far off in his assessment.

"It figures that that coward Mayor Price ran and hid when people started getting mad," I muttered as Briggs pulled me through the maze of black suits and silk dresses. "Who knew Port Danby people had such finery in their closets," I said on a near whisper.

We reached the entrance of the tent. "There's Briggs," someone said over the other voices, "he'll get to the bottom of this."

I giggled. "I feel so important being dragged along like a kite behind the famous James Briggs."

Briggs squeezed my hand and dragged me closer behind him. "Not sure what they expect me to do. Whip out my badge and demand they start the play?" A troubled looking stagehand stepped around the side of the tent and then, with a look of horror at the scene in front of it, spun around and took off.

"That's not exactly an encouraging sign," Briggs said. He released my hand and took off after the guy. I stood in the center of the irritated crowd and smiled at a few of the lingering, scrutinizing gazes.

"She runs the local flower shop," I heard someone mutter not so quietly behind me. There were definitely faces I didn't recognize, people from Mayfield and Chesterton, no doubt.

I breathed a sigh of relief when Briggs came back around the tent. "Well, Briggs," someone shouted. "What's going on? We're all freezing. Either they should let us in or they should refund our money."

"One of the cast members is missing. They're looking for her now," Briggs explained.

"Well, if it's just one cast member, why don't they get on with it and work the play around her?" someone asked.

Briggs had an amused glint in his eyes as his gaze swept past me. "Because the missing cast member is Dorothy."

Grunts mingled with a few gasps and an even fewer giggles. My reaction landed somewhere between the two. *The Wizard of Oz* couldn't very well go on without Dorothy. I wondered if her absence had anything to do with the terrible fight she'd had with Susana. Maybe she was trying to put a little scare into the director to remind her how important her role was and that the show couldn't go on without her.

"Will they give us our money back?" someone shouted over the heads.

"How did I get thrown into this mess?" Briggs said quietly.

The disgruntled growls in the crowd grew louder, but the entire group fell silent when a scream cut through the night air. People glanced anxiously around.

Briggs looked at me. "Did that come from the tent?"

"That's what I was thinking."

"Help, I think she's dead!" a voice yelled from inside the tent.

Briggs grabbed my hand. Startled onlookers stepped aside as he pushed his way to the tent entrance. He pulled open the flap and we stepped inside. Props were set up to display a farm scene, only the house that I'd seen them carry in earlier was face down on the stage. A shaken looking stagehand, a young man whose face looked as pale as the tent canvas, was pointing down at something.

Briggs and I raced to the stage. More of the theater group, stagehands, extras and a few of the play attendees crowded into the tent behind us. We reached the stage and froze at the sight of a pair of thin legs clad in black patent leather shoes sticking out from the fallen house.

My first reaction was that it was some sort of prank. "Isn't the house supposed to fall on the witch?" I asked, then realized the stagehand's face was dead serious.

Briggs didn't take time to walk around to the stage steps. He hauled himself up on stage. (I, on the other hand, decided to walk up the stairs.) Briggs and the stagehand had lifted the wooden prop up to its proper position before I reached the body.

"Dorothy," I said on a gasped breath. She was pale and lifeless. A gray cable was wrapped around her neck, and the skin beneath it was bright red.

Briggs knelt down next to the body and quickly unwrapped the cable. I knew from his unhurried movements that he was certain she was dead. He pressed his fingers near the red mark on her neck and searched for a pulse. A minute later he glanced up at me and flashed the look that confirmed my suspicions.

Briggs stood up and turned to the stagehand. It was then that we both noticed he looked close to passing out. "One of you come up here and escort this man down to a chair. He needs to put his head between his knees," Briggs said. "I'll need the rest of you to clear out and find me the person in charge of this operation."

A trembling voice spoke up from behind the theater crew. "That's me." Susana pushed weakly through the group. "What's happened?" She hurried to the stage and peered up onto it. Her face and lips went white. "Amanda," she looked urgently at Briggs. "Is she sick? I'll call for an ambulance."

Briggs shook his head. "I'll take care of this. Just get everyone out."

For a moment I could see why Susana wasn't exactly stellar in her director's position. She stood stock-still with a dumbfounded look, seemingly not sure what to do.

One brave crew member, a tall, well-built woman with a tool belt around her hips, broke free of the stunned group. "Kevin, get everyone out of here." She continued on toward the stage to retrieve her sickly looking stagehand. "Bobby, I'm on my way. Don't faint."

"Thank you, Patty," Susana uttered weakly. She'd pulled herself out of a trance but wasn't much more help.

Patty managed to get to Bobby and pried him from the spot his feet had frozen to. She led him down the stairs to the audience area and sat him firmly in a chair. Briggs had walked to the back of the stage to make a call. I was sure he was calling his evidence team and the coroner, but he wasn't ready to distress the flustered director with all that shocking information.

The tent was cleared. Briggs finished his calls and walked down the steps to talk to Susana. He placed a bracing hand under her elbow and walked her away from the stage, so Amanda's body was out of view. I was left alone on the platform with the victim dressed prettily in her gingham pinafore and shiny leather shoes. And, in this case, there was no doubt that she was indeed a victim . . . a victim of murder.

CHAPTER 12

he coroner will be here soon," Briggs said as he reached me on the stage. Like the wobbly kneed Bobby, Susana had to be helped out of the tent for some fresh air. On top of the terrible tragedy, she now had to contend with a cold, angry audience who had been waiting in the wet fog for a play they were never going to see. Briggs told her to wait for his backup team before delivering the bad news. Not that he expected anyone to get unruly but you never knew, and the crowd had reached somewhat of a boiling point. It would be harder and less feasible to get unruly when wearing your nicest clothes.

"Do you think you can do a proper nasal inspection before Nate's team arrives?" Briggs asked.

I had to suppress a frown. "Do you doubt my abilities?"

"No, no"—he shook his head—"definitely not that. I just thought your head cold might be an obstacle to a proper sniff around."

"I suppose that makes sense." I tapped my nose. "Samantha might be in a bit of a fog, but I'm sure I'll be able to detect any odors that are out of place."

I took off my scarf and handed it to him before kneeling down next to Amanda. She was on her back with one hand on her stomach and the other fallen to her side. Both hands were empty. It was easy to see the red line on the fingertips of the hand resting at her side. She had fought off her attacker but failed.

"Before I start, I want to point out this long piece of straw in her left pigtail. Just in case it moves or something as I hover over her."

"I saw that earlier. Thanks for the reminder." Briggs walked over and took a picture of the straw.

I peered up at him. "The Scarecrow has a great deal of straw on his costume, and I know a few things about the relationships and dynamics between the cast members."

"I would expect nothing less from you," he said with a tempered smile (due to the situation).

I leaned down over Amanda's face and instantly sat up with a sneeze. I'd barely pulled my tissue out in time before it exploded.

"Bless you," Briggs said. "The cold? Or something else?"

"There's only one way to find out." I held my breath, leaned low, took a cautious sniff and sneezed again. "Definitely something near her neck area that is making me sneeze. I'm getting a slight scent of it but not exactly sure what yet. I hope it doesn't make my nasal inspection impossible." I pushed to my feet. "Let me move to the other side. I think the scent is coming from the right side of her neck."

As I knelt down, something sparkly caught my eye. "Glitter," I mumbled.

"What's that?" Briggs asked. He'd just finished a text and put the phone in his pocket.

I pointed at Amanda's cheek. The skin was pale beneath the exaggerated pink cheek circles the makeup artist had added. "There are a few pieces of glitter clinging to her face." I drew my gaze along her neck, shoulders and dress. Bits of glitter sparkled up from various locations all over the victim.

Instinctively, Briggs and I surveyed the set. Glitter was not a part of the set decoration, yet there seemed to be bits of it everywhere, even on the stage floor and the tent canvas.

"I suppose it probably doesn't mean much because glitter is one of those substances that is pervasive like crabgrass in a front lawn. I once sprinkled glitter on a fourth grade art project. That glittery project haunted us for months. My mom was seriously ready to sell the house just to get away from the glitter."

Briggs laughed quietly as he reached for his buzzing phone. "You might be right about it being insignificant. But we'll collect some as evidence."

"The Munchkin costumes were adorned in glitter, so that might be why it's everywhere. You know how they like to dance around and sing," I quipped before remembering the somber task in front of me.

Briggs answered the phone. "Briggs here."

The fabric of her costume, Dorothy's iconic pinafore, smelled mostly of laundry detergent and starch. It made my nose tickle, but that could also have been from the mystery scent that caused me to sneeze. I was far enough away from it to avoid a sneeze fit.

I'd always found the hands revealed the most of what the person had been up to hours before. This time was no different. Amanda's injured fingers curled lightly in toward her palm. My guess would have been that she ate a tuna salad sandwich for lunch.

I could hear the coroner's deep voice rumble through the tent as my nose hovered over her fingers. Briggs jumped off the stage to greet him and fill him in on details.

Nate Blankenship's arrival was the reminder for me to finish up. I stopped mid-sniff and lingered over one particular spot on her arm. "Rosemary," I said to myself. "The Tin Man smelled like rosemary too."

Nate stopped to give instructions to his two assistants. Briggs joined me after giving the evidence team a few directions. He gave me a hand up. "Anything interesting?" he asked.

"I think she ate a tuna sandwich for lunch. Have you ever had a tuna sandwich that contained rosemary?"

He looked rightly confused. "I'm not too well versed on tuna sandwich recipes, but I think I'd remember if I ate one with rosemary."

"That's what I was thinking. I smell rosemary on her forearm. Seems out of place. Just like it was out of place when I smelled it on the Tin Man this afternoon."

Briggs rubbed his chin, something he did when he was thinking or highly puzzled. "Why on earth were you sniffing the Tin Man this afternoon? Are you sure you're not just smelling the remnants of our ravioli dinner?"

I lowered my face to look pointedly at him. "I would know if I was smelling the remnants of our dinner because there would be a decent amount of garlic and oregano involved."

"Pardon me for questioning the master nose. Let's get to the first part of my bewilderment. Why were you smelling the Tin Man?"

"It was quite accidental, I assure you," I started, then we were motioned away from the area as the coroner crew moved in. Briggs and I walked down the steps to the floor of the tent where rows and rows of chairs had been neatly arranged for the audience. I could still hear a plethora of noise and conversations outside the canvas walls. I could only assume members of the theater group were standing around in the gray fog consoling each other and waiting for questions to be answered. It was also easy to assume that Amanda's killer was standing amongst them. After all, who else would have had access to the tent except members of the cast or crew.

"I need to interview some of the group so fill me in on the Tin Man and anything else you already know." Briggs pulled out his notepad.

"I was heading back to Pickford Way after leaving the mayor's office. Just after I hung up with you, I walked around one of the theater trailers and ran sort of smack dab into the Tin Man, in full makeup and costume. And let me tell you that man's hubris was not muted by the silver makeup, boxy costume and funnel hat. He was very forward," I added but quickly decided I should not have gone off on that particular tangent.

Briggs' eyes narrowed. "What did he do?" He then shook his head. "Probably better I don't know before I interview him."

"Smart thinking. Anyhow, I think his name is Johnny. A crew member called him while I was talking to him. After our near collision, I smelled tobacco and rosemary. I decided to ask if the two were related." I shrugged. "Thought maybe it had been some kind of herbal cigarette, but it turned out that Tom and Gigi ran out of regular oil at the Corner Market so the prop crew filled his oil can with rosemary infused olive oil. That's what I smelled mingled with the pungent tobacco. I just happened to have smelled a light amount of it on Dorothy. I mean Amanda."

Briggs dashed off a few notes. "Guess I should interview Tin Man. But first I'm going to talk to the director and find out the schedule and logistics of the group during the last few hours. She was still slightly warm when I felt for a pulse, so she was killed just a short time ago."

"Good idea and you might ask Susana about the fight she had with Amanda this afternoon."

We headed toward the exit. The entire tent was lit up with Nate's bright lights. They put up a screen around their examination area.

Briggs stopped so short, I had to back up a few steps.

"What fight?"

"On my walk to the mayor's office, an excursion that is proving more and more fruitful by the minute, I overheard Susana and Amanda having a very loud fight. According to Tin Man, they rarely saw eye to eye. Even though Susana was the director, it sure seemed that Amanda had the upper hand in the fight."

He wrote down a few notes, stuck his pen behind his ear and shook his head.

"What would you do without me?" I asked airily.

He held open the tent flap. "I'd find a new profession."

CHAPTER 13

*O*nce we were outside the protection of the tent, the frosty air reminded me that I was under the weather. The aspirin had temporarily put me back on my feet, but as the chilly, damp air seeped through clothes and skin, some of my aches and chills had returned. Briggs was always so tuned into my mood that he knew instantly the cold weather was getting to me.

"Lacey, I'll have one of the officers drive you home. You shouldn't be out here in this damp ocean air. You've already been helpful enough, and you know I'll fill you in on any details tomorrow."

I was close to accepting his offer, then I saw Susana heading toward one of the trailers. She was dragging her feet as if heavy stones had been wrapped around her ankles. Her head hung low, and she had her director's cap pulled far down over her face.

"I want to hear what the director has to say. Then maybe I'll take you up on the ride home."

He scrutinized me with his caring brown gaze. It helped warm me a bit from the inside. "If you're sure."

"I am. I saw her go into that white and gray trailer." I pointed across to the line of trailers parked on Pickford Way. We headed that direction.

It seemed most of the theater group, actors and crew members had wandered into warm trailers to finish processing the terrible opening night. Word had gotten to Briggs that a group wanted to walk over to Franki's Diner for some coffee and to commiserate about the tragedy. He gave his approval but mentioned that everyone was to stay in town and near the theater camp.

Haze seemed to bounce out of the cold, dewy lawn as our feet tromped across it. The fog was heavy enough to obliterate natural light from the stars and moon, but the lighthouse swung her beautiful warning light around to illuminate the area.

Briggs had his notepad and pen ready as we climbed the steps to the trailer door. He knocked. "It's Detective Briggs. I'd like to ask you a few questions."

The door opened slowly, and Susana peered around the edge of the door. "Detective Briggs, I figured you'd come see me. I'm sorry if I seem weary. It's been a long night. I'm afraid I sent away a lot of angry, disappointed folks. Please come inside, and excuse the mess. I was helping with some of the costumes this evening."

Several brightly colored blouses with glittered trim, the Munchkin outfits, were hanging from a rack in the center of the small living area. The tiny sofa was littered with script pages that had been highlighted and marked up with red pen. An empty cracker box and half empty bottle of root beer sat on a fold-up television table. Susana leaned over and snatched up the various script sheets. She placed them on the tiny kitchen table next to an open laptop. "Please have a seat."

"No need for that. We won't be long. I appreciate that you've been through a great deal of stress tonight so I'll keep it brief," Briggs said. "It's Ms. Damon, right? By the way, this is my assistant, Miss Pinkerton."

She nodded and had the funny look people wore when they

were trying to remember when and where they'd seen someone before. "Yes, Susana is fine," she said.

Briggs and I found a small clearing to stand in. "First of all, could you give me a brief summary of what was happening on this site in the last four hours. Lots of activity, I imagine?"

Susana glanced toward her coffee pot. The light was on. "I'm afraid I only made one cup," she said. "Do you mind if I pour it? I could make more."

"No, we're fine," Briggs answered for both of us though hot coffee did sound nice. "Please have your coffee," he added politely. Briggs was an expert at making people feel at ease with his questioning. Sometimes people grew instantly defensive, but Susana seemed much more relaxed than earlier this evening.

She plucked a cup from the cupboard. "You asked about the schedule." She reached across the sink and picked up a clipboard. "I have it right here. The prop crew erected the various sets on the stage from one until three. The cast was in makeup and costume at that time. That's when the full cast assembled in the tent for a director's pep talk and the dress rehearsal." She flipped over a page. "Dress rehearsal started at ten past three and ended at half past four. It went smoothly." She stopped and took a wavering breath. "Everyone was on time for their cues, props held up and only a few lines were missed. I considered it a good omen for opening night. We're very superstitious in this business. But I was wrong." Her voice cracked with the last sentence. "I'm sorry." She sniffled and took a sip of coffee.

Susana was in the business of acting and drama, so it would be hard to see through fake emotion but this looked pretty genuine.

Briggs wrote down all the pertinent times and notations, then he looked up. "Where did you go after the dress rehearsal? Did you happen to see Miss Seton, the victim?"

The simple question flustered her more than I would have

thought. I knew my partner well enough to know he was making a mental note of the reaction too.

Susana took another sip of coffee, then placed the cup on the counter. "I asked Amanda to stay after dress rehearsal. I needed to talk to her." She seemed to be searching for the right way to explain her meeting with Amanda. Was she avoiding trying to sound guilty or looking for an innocent explanation? It was hard to tell. Drama people, I thought with a mental scoff.

Briggs looked up to let her know he was waiting for her to continue.

She reached for her coffee cup. It had seemingly become her security blanket. She cleared her throat. "Earlier in the day, Amanda and I had exchanged a few terse words," she confessed.

Terse was not exactly the descriptor I would have used for the fight I'd witnessed. She was tempering her confession.

"Terse words?" Briggs repeated as a question. Of course, Susana had no way of knowing that Briggs already knew she'd had a fight with Amanda.

It was apparent that even *she* was uncomfortable with her choice of word after hearing it repeated aloud.

She sighed. "Amanda Seton and I did not see eye to eye all the time. Even though I'm the director, she felt that her position as lead actress made her invulnerable to being replaced or told no. She insisted on special treatment all the time. For the most part, I was willing to grant her privileges, but some of the other cast members were growing resentful. Whenever I tried to explain that to her, she'd fly off the handle. She had quite the temper." Susana paused and stared down at the smudged linoleum floor. "I can't believe I'm using the past tense when talking about her."

Briggs gave her a moment to collect herself. We exchanged glances. It seemed we were both trying to assess whether or not the emotion was an act.

Susana lifted her face. It was mottled with splotches that led me to believe the show of emotion was real. "Anyhow, we had a fairly tense argument before dress rehearsal. I felt compelled to be the first person to apologize. Sometimes the boss has to take that initiative," she continued. "While she was off set, I texted her a quick message to remain behind in the tent once the dress rehearsal finished. It was the only quiet place I could think of."

Briggs glanced pointedly around her trailer. "With the exception of this trailer."

"No," she said too abruptly. "This place is rarely my sanctuary. As you can see by the clutter and smudges on the floor, there are constantly people traipsing through here or knocking at the door to talk to me. It's quiet now only because of what's happened. I told people I needed to be alone for a bit."

Briggs nodded. "Fine. So you chose the tent as your meeting place. Everyone else had cleared out?" he asked.

"Yes. There was only an hour for dinner before we needed to get ready for the opening so people took off."

"And Amanda stayed behind?" Briggs asked.

"Yes. We spoke briefly so she wouldn't miss her break. I apologized and told her after opening tonight we would sit down and make a list of some of her requests, and I'd let her know which ones were feasible."

"Requests?" Briggs asked.

She shrugged. "Simple things like a special herbal tea that she liked to have with breakfast and a twice a week massage. She liked to be pampered. I didn't mind as long as it was in the budget and it didn't upset the others. There were things like a personal chef that I had to say no to, of course. She would get angry but then eventually she'd let it go. This afternoon she insisted I do something about the stage lighting because it made her look yellowish. It was a technical request that I told her would take a work order and a discussion with the lighting crew. She wanted it done for opening night, and I told her that wasn't possible. She got very angry."

"So the words exchanged earlier might have been a good degree more than terse?" Briggs asked. Sometimes I marveled at how subtle yet pressing he could be.

Susana nodded. "I suppose terse wasn't the right word. But I assure you, all was well after my apology and our chat. I left the tent and didn't speak to her again." That statement produced another long pause of sad reflection.

"Did you see her leave the tent?" Briggs asked.

She was genuinely puzzled by the question. Her eyes rolled up to the side. "Let me think. I walked toward my trailer so my back was toward the tent, but she didn't walk out with me. She was still sitting in the chair she'd taken for our discussion when I left the tent."

"Did you have dinner with anyone or talk to anyone after your discussion with Amanda?" I knew Briggs' question would put her on the defensive, but sometimes there just wasn't any way to be subtle. He needed an alibi and usually that called for more directness.

Susana's feet fidgeted on the vinyl floor causing her rubber soled shoes to make a loud noise. "I came to this trailer and heated myself a frozen dinner. The empty tray is in the trash if you need to see proof." Her tone was much sharper.

"No, I don't need to see it." Briggs always kept his cool. (One of the gazillion things I loved about him.) "So you ate dinner alone? Who did you speak to next?"

"I took a little rest on my couch and waited for dinner break to end. It had been such an exhausting day, I dozed off. The sound of urgent knocking woke me. That was when Wendall, the casting assistant, let me know that Amanda hadn't returned from dinner. He was lining the cast up to check that costumes and makeup hadn't been messed up during the break, but Amanda was nowhere to be found. No one had seen her."

Briggs finished writing in his notepad and put it away. "Thank you for your time, Ms. Damon. We'll let you know if we need anything else."

"How long will it take for the police to be finished? My crew and cast are going to be tired after all this."

"It should be another hour or so. We're going to talk to a few more people too. Again, thanks for your time."

We walked out of the trailer.

"Ready to head home?" he asked.

"I'm not feeling too bad. I'd like to stick around a little longer if that's all right."

"I figured you'd say that." He curled his arm around my shoulders and gave me a little squeeze. It was all I needed to feel better.

CHAPTER 14

*B*riggs stopped at the tent where both the coroner and the evidence team were finishing up. Amanda's body had already been zipped into a body bag and lifted into the coroner's van. Nate's assistants were just picking up equipment. I waited at the entrance to the tent while he was debriefed. I pulled the long end of my knitted scarf so that it covered my shoulders like a shawl, and I tugged the warm wool up over my chin, nearly covering my mouth. Standing there in the cold mist, I thought it might be a good idea for me to head home to bed. Then I saw Gordon with his clumsy, heavy footed gait walking along the path to the tent. There were a few people with him. At least two of them carried the white bags Franki handed out for leftovers. Briggs had mentioned that several of the theater group members were going to head to the diner for coffee. Even after a tragedy, it would take willpower to sit in Franki's Diner and just have coffee. Seeing Gordon reminded me of the straw and the interesting nuggets I'd discovered about the Scarecrow throughout the day.

Briggs reached me just as I finished my mental decision to stick out the night air a little longer. "I noticed you've practically cocooned yourself into that scarf. Are you sure you don't want to head home?"

"I'll stay around for one more interview, one that might just be too interesting to miss." I looked toward the tall figure lumbering toward us. "That's Gordon, the actor who plays the Scarecrow."

"Ah ha, the guy with all the straw," he said quietly. "Nate found a second piece of straw on the back of the victim's hair too. Near the nape of her neck."

"I have to speak quickly because he's getting closer, but he came into my store this morning with Constance, his girlfriend. She plays some of the minor parts. But later in the day, Elsie mentioned that the Scarecrow and Dorothy, our victim, came into the bakery. They were in full costume, probably just before dress rehearsal. Elsie was tickled by it all because she said they were flirting and then she went into this whole speech about Dorothy having a tryst with one of her three companions," I shook my head. "Not important," I said just as Gordon passed us.

"Uh, Gordon," Briggs said quickly.

Gordon stopped and nodded goodnight to the others as they continued on to the trailers. His brows bunched up. There were still smears of makeup here and there on his face. His eyebrows were still kohl black, a stark difference from his light blond hair. Even under the streaks of leftover makeup and the dim lights around the tent, his face looked drawn, like someone who had suffered a serious blow. The pained expression caused me a twinge of guilt for thinking that he might very well be the killer. I also had to remind myself that he was an actor, but was it really that simple to portray anguish?

Briggs showed him his badge. "Detective Briggs, Mr.—" he paused for Gordon to supply the name.

"Houser, Gordon Houser. Did they find out who did this?" There was a nice touch of vengeful anger in his tone. Was he acting? This case was going to be harder than usual because reactions and emotions were all going to have to be taken with a spoonful of skepticism.

"Not yet but we will," Briggs said confidently. He shot me a wink. It was a partner wink. (Not just a measly assistant wink.) Then he went right on to introduce me as his assistant.

"This is Miss Pinkerton, my assistant. I wonder if we could step into the tent where it's a little warmer? I just want to ask you a few questions."

He nodded weakly. "I suppose but I'm tired. It's been a big shock."

"I understand. We won't keep you long." Briggs pushed open the flap and the three of us stepped inside. There was more lighting inside the tent, which allowed Gordon to get a better look at the *assistant*.

His thickly drawn, Groucho Marx style brows looked comical when bunched. "Aren't you the florist? I bought some roses from you this morning."

"Yes, that was me. I have a part time position assisting Detective Briggs." Of course, my explanation was weird and a little hard to believe. Sometimes, I could hardly believe it.

"I see," he said in a tone that assured me he didn't. He turned to Briggs. "What did you need to ask me? Amanda was a great gal and a terrific actress. This group might not survive without her."

"Yes, that's clear. I'm sorry for you loss," Briggs said as he pulled out his notepad. Everyone reacted differently to his very unpretentious notebook. Gordon was clearly taken aback that a detective would be writing down some of his statements.

"Is this an interrogation?" Gordon asked.

"I'm just gathering as many details of today's activities as I can. It will help me sort out people, places and times which, in turn, will help me find the killer."

Gordon's face blanched under the ruddy makeup smeared on his cheeks. "So she was definitely murdered?"

"Nothing is definite until we get the coroner's report, but it looks like foul play."

Gordon scrubbed his fingers in his shaggy hair. "I don't understand who would do such a thing. What do you need from me? I want to help." His attitude had done an about face.

"When was the last time you saw Miss Seton?" Briggs asked.

He scrubbed his hair again, only this time it was a ploy to earn him some time. "Well, let me see." A long pause followed. It was long enough to feel awkward. I glanced casually around, letting him search for his answer, but Briggs stayed unflinching with his gaze straight on the man and his pen at the ready.

"I guess it was when the two of us went to town. We were dressed and ready. As main characters, we have priority in hair and makeup. We had an hour to kill." He dropped his face. "Bad choice of word." His chest spread out with a deep, steadying breath. "Amanda and I decided to get a treat at the bakery." His face turned my direction. "I'd noticed how wonderful the place smelled when I came to your flower shop in the morning, so I thought it would be a nice place to get a snack."

I nodded. "It's hard to resist Elsie's baked goods. Did Constance join you two on your trip to the bakery?"

My question pushed him into a short, red-faced stutter session. "Con-Constance uh—uh—no she was in makeup at that time," he said the latter with a relieved breath. Apparently, he was pleased with himself for coming up with a good excuse for sharing lemon tarts with someone other than his steady girlfriend. Elsie, who was a keen observer, was certain Gordon and Amanda were flirting heavily with one another. She was tickled about the prospect of Dorothy and the Scarecrow having a fling.

Gordon decided he hadn't given enough explanation. "Like I said, Amanda and I were waiting for the extras to get ready for dress rehearsal. We just decided to take a short walk through town. Susie likes us to make brief appearances in costume in the towns we're playing in. It's good advertising. It was just a trip to the bakery. Nothing else." It was a short confession that was pointed at the wrong audience. He could have saved it for Constance.

I sensed Briggs was getting tired of the interview when he got straight to the next point. "Your costume is designed to make you look as if you're made of straw, correct?"

"Yes, that's right." Gordon didn't seem to have a clue where the questioning was headed, but I knew exactly what Briggs would ask next.

"We found several pieces of straw in the victim's hair. One piece was lodged in the hair near the base of her neck. Any idea how it might have gotten there?"

Gordon's face reddened. "Should I have a lawyer here?"

His stern question tossed Briggs slightly off his game but he recovered quickly. "You're certainly entitled to have one with you. Not accusing you of anything. Just wondering how the straw got in her hair."

He fidgeted with the belt on his pants and shuffled his big feet a bit. Then his face brightened as if a teeny, tiny light bulb had just flashed on in his brain. "The sun was getting lower on our walk back from the bakery. Amanda was just wearing a thin cotton dress. She got cold, so I pulled off my costume coat and put it around her shoulders." He motioned to one of the trailers. "The coat is hanging in the costume trailer if you want to see it. Straw is glued around the collar and cuffs to make it look like my stuffing is coming out," he added with a wry smile. He was quite pleased with himself for coming up with a perfectly reasonable explanation for Amanda having straw in her hair. "You can go look at it. That stuff is a mess. There's a pile of straw right below where my costume hangs." He rubbed the back of his neck. "It makes me itch too. I'm sure some of it got stuck in Amanda's hair while she was wearing my coat."

It was an entirely plausible explanation, but he certainly wasn't willing to admit that there was more to the bakery trip than a quest for one of Elsie's tarts.

Briggs finished his notes and looked up. "What happened after the trip to the bakery?"

Gordon stopped to think a moment. "Amanda and I parted when we reached the town square. She was going to practice her lines and have some tea. I went to my trailer to rest until dress rehearsal. I didn't see her again until we were on stage rehearsing."

"And after rehearsal?" Briggs was wasting no time gathering possible alibis.

He groaned quietly. "It's been a long, trying night. I'm not sure."

"It would be helpful if you could remember," Briggs prodded.

"Fine, I went back to my trailer and had a few shots of whiskey. It helps me relax before being on stage."

"And then?" Briggs asked.

"I fell asleep. Guess it helps me relax a little too much. One of the crew came and woke me when it was close to show time. Never saw Amanda after rehearsal." His mouth turned down at the sides. "I never would have guessed that would be our last time on stage together."

The salt laden fog that had settled over the coast had started to seep beneath the tent. I shivered once, imperceptibly, I thought, but Briggs caught it. He put his notepad away.

"Thank you very much, Mr. Houser. I'll let you know if there's anything else we need. Go get some rest. I'm sure it's been an exhausting few hours."

Gordon nodded. "Just find the person fast. None of us are going to get a good night's sleep with a killer on the loose." He walked out of the tent.

We listened for his heavy footsteps to retreat, then Briggs took hold of my hand.

"You need to get home now, and I won't take no for an answer."

"You don't have to worry. I don't have any 'no' to give. Do you think you'll be here long tonight?"

"No, in fact I'll drive you home. The theater group is exhausted and still in shock. Sometimes people have better recollections after a good night of sleep."

A yawn escaped me before I could suppress it.

"Let's get you home, Miss Pinkerton."

"Sounds like a grand idea, Detective Briggs."

CHAPTER 15

*B*riggs walked me inside the house. He headed straight into the kitchen to put the kettle on for some tea. I shuffled to the bedroom and pulled on my favorite flannel pajamas and thickest pair of socks.

A steaming cup of chamomile tea was waiting for me as I reached the kitchen. I cupped it between my hands to warm them. Briggs pressed his hand against my forehead.

I peered up at him from the shade of his palm. "Does that really work? I'm not convinced. I would tell my mom I was too sick with fever to go to school, and she'd slap her hand against my forehead and seconds later tell me I was fine.

Briggs lowered his hand and chuckled. "My mom did the exact same thing. I tried to convince her that her palm was colder than it should be and that's why she couldn't feel the fever. But you, my sweet angel, definitely feel warm."

I smiled up at him. "Any girl would feel warm with Detective James Briggs calling her his sweet angel. I normally don't need this kind of affirmation, but I'm feeling crummy so say it again, please."

He took gentle hold of both my arms and kissed my forehead. "My sweet angel. Now drink tea and go to bed."

"I plan to." I pointed at him. "Don't go back out there and find the killer before I get a chance to sink my teeth into this one. There are all kinds of interesting characters involved. In every sense of the word."

"Fine, I'll just push my job aside for now," he said wryly.

"Don't tease. I'm feverish and wearing flannel and fluffy socks. Tomorrow, I'll be right as rain and ready to solve the case."

"I hope so," he said as he reached the door. He glanced back over his shoulder with those rich brown eyes. "I don't know how much longer I can go without kissing those lips." With that he walked out, leaving me a touch breathless.

I pulled my phone from my coat pocket. I hadn't checked it at all during the chaos of the night. There were two missed calls from Lola. I was tired and it was after ten, but I knew Lola stayed up late. It was unusual for her to call and not text. She must have heard about the disastrous opening night. I was sure the whole town knew already. I hadn't seen Mayor Price all evening. It would be just like him to hide at home to avoid the mess.

Lola left no voicemail so I quickly deduced it wasn't anything too important. I was sure she just wanted to hear about the awful night, and I was too tired to give a proper account of the events. She would have to wait until tomorrow, then I could relay the whole thing to Ryder, Lola and anyone else who was interested.

Nevermore had curled up on my pillow. He had an incredibly soft mattress covered by my downy quilt to use as a cat nest, but it wasn't luxurious enough for my spoiled feline. He wanted the pillow. I nudged him off. He got up lazily, like a bear being woken from hibernation. Before vacating my pillow, he went into a series of yoga stretches that would impress even the most intense yoga instructor. He kneaded my cotton pillowcase a few times with his paws, making sure to leave some tiny claw holes in the fabric before finally strolling down to the foot of the bed.

I flipped my pillow over and propped it up against the head-board so I could finish my tea. It was lukewarm now but it felt good on my throat and it helped clear my stuffy nose. I was savoring the last few drops when my phone startled me, causing the tea cup to clatter against my teeth. I rubbed them as if teeth had feeling and answered the phone.

"Hey, Lola, guess you heard about the crazy night at the theater."

"What crazy night?"

"The murder? The actress who played Dorothy was found dead. And get this—the house fell on her, but that didn't kill her. A laptop cable was found wrapped around her neck." I'd inadvertently called it a laptop cable even though I wasn't sure.

"Isn't the house supposed to fall on the witch?" she asked.

I nodded to myself. "And that is why we are best friends."

"*Were* best friends, you mean," she said.

"What do you mean? We're not friends anymore?"

"I suppose I won't delete your name from my contacts," she said with a snooty tone. "But best friends tell best friends when they know something big and life changing."

"I guess Ryder finally told you about his research opportunity in the Amazon." I rested back against my pillow. My eyelids and head felt heavy.

"What? No? He's going to the Amazon?" she asked frantically. "I was calling because Elsie isn't going to make cinnamon rolls on Monday."

I sat forward. "Oh no. You mean Ryder didn't talk to you?" The sickness moved down to my stomach. "Lola, I'm sor—"

Her evil giggle floated through the phone. "There. A little revenge for you not telling me the second you knew that my boyfriend was going to desert me for some exotic vacation."

I collapsed back in relief. "You are a mean best friend, and I might just delete *you* from my contacts. How could you do that when I've been sick all day and then there was the whole dead Dorothy thing and all? And he's not going on an exotic vacation. It's for research. It'll be a great opportunity for him. Besides, you might be without a boyfriend, but they say absence makes the heart grow fonder. I'll be without my stellar assistant. And right in the middle of bridal season."

"That's that then, I'll just tell him to stay home," she said flatly. "He told me he wouldn't go if I was upset about it."

I paused and let her rethink what she said.

"Of course I can't tell him to stay home. Like you said, it's a great opportunity, and I don't want to get in the way of his career."

"Smart girl," I said. "You're back in my contact list. Even though I've probably aged a few years with your little prank. By the way, you were only kidding about the cinnamon rolls, weren't you?"

Another crafty sounding giggle. "Maybe or maybe not. Guess it'll be a long Sunday night while you contemplate that question. So—Dorothy is dead? I guess *the show didn't go on* as they say."

"No it didn't. I stuck around for the investigation, but the fog was extra miserable down by the beach, so I was happy to get home to my flannel pajamas and my bed."

"Did I wake you?" she asked.

"No, I was just finishing my tea."

"I suppose I should let you sleep then." There was a touch of sadness in her voice.

"Hey, the time will fly, and just think of all the cool stories Ryder will have for us when he gets back. Besides, you have me to hang out with."

"You'll have no time for me. You'll be creating entire bridal arrangements all on your own."

"Maybe you can learn floral arranging in the meantime," I suggested just before yawning into the phone.

"Great, Ryder hasn't left and you're already bored with me. Go to sleep and get rid of this cold. I'm tired of looking at that red nose."

"I could powder it."

"Good night," Lola said.

"Good night." I put the phone on the dresser. I flicked off the light, scooted down into the cozy sanctuary of my bed and fell fast asleep.

CHAPTER 16

Nevermore woke me from a dream where I was building a model boat with a flying monkey. Then the monkey morphed into a cinnamon roll, and I ate him while sitting on a spinning tea cup. I shook it all from my head and realized, at once, that I was feeling better. Not a hundred percent but much better than the night before.

I had a good two hours before I needed to open the shop. I climbed out of bed and walked to the kitchen to feed Nevermore. There was no use trying to fall back asleep with a hungry cat hovering over me.

My phone rang the second I reached the kitchen. I had to race back to the bedroom to pluck it off my nightstand. I was expecting it to be Briggs with new information about the case but the screen said Mom. She occasionally liked to call before I left for work.

"Hello," I said as I quickly spun around to go back to the kitchen

"You have a cold," she said.

"How could you tell that with one word?"

"You sound very nasal."

"That's lovely to know." Nevermore swirled around the flannel legs of my pajamas, producing a good amount of static with his fur, as I reached up to the cupboard for his bag of food.

"You should make yourself some chicken soup." I was sure it was only the first of a litany of suggestions about how to take care of myself. (I would remain forever a kid in her mind.)

"I don't have time to make chicken soup. I already had some of Franki's and, while comforting, it isn't quite the miracle cure you moms purport it to be."

"What was I reading the other day?" she trailed off to have a chat with herself. "Oh yes, warm compresses that have been soaked in green tea. I read it someplace on the internet."

"Yes, well, did this rich, invaluable source also tell you where to place the compresses?" I poured the cat's food.

She paused. "Can't remember." Dad's voice drifted through the phone. He was having his usual background sidebar with her while we talked.

"I think I'll skip the compresses. I'm feeling better anyhow." I headed over to Kingston's cage and pulled off the fabric cover that provided him with artificial night. He was already bright eyed and pacing his perch for breakfast. I opened his cage. He climbed out and sat on top of it. Dad muttered something in the background. I tried to interpret what he was saying.

"I thought I heard Dad say something about eating fresh vegetables. Has he finally come around to the benefit of eating things that are green?"

"Oh, heavens no. I still have to coat his broccoli with cheese sauce. It's like feeding a six-year-old. No, he's talking about the llama."

"The llama?" I asked not sure I'd heard right. "Did you say llama? Oh my gosh, I'm going to be so mad if you finally got a cool pet after I begged you for a raccoon like the Meyersons had."

"That raccoon was ghastly and mean," she reminded me. It was true but it didn't stop me from wanting one.

"Never mind about that. What about the llama?" I headed back to the kitchen to make coffee.

Mom made a puffed sound. "Your father wants a pet llama because he read somewhere on the internet that some people use them as caddies on the golf course."

A laugh caused me to spill coffee on the counter. I grabbed a towel to clean it up. "I can just see Dad now walking to the first hole with his big fuzzy llama carrying his golf clubs in a pack on his back. That would either impress his golf buddies, or they'd be dialing the funny farm to come cart him away. Exactly where would he keep his new golf caddy? The den?"

"Obviously he's going to have to give up on the idea, but he has spent the last three days researching how to care for a llama," Mom scoffed.

"You two need some hobbies that don't include reading things on the internet."

"Anyhow, I was just calling to tell you we're traveling to see Aunt Millie for a few days in case you need us."

"That's nice. Give her a hug for me. And you realize that if I do need you, I'll still be calling this same number, so it really doesn't matter where you are as long as your phone is with you."

"Yes, I knew that, smarty pants" she said with some bluster. "I just thought you'd like to know where we were."

There was a knock on the door. "Yes and thank you for that. Have a safe trip, Mom. I've got to go."

"All right and don't forget the tea compresses and chicken soup," she reminded as she hung up.

I peeked through the peephole, even though I was fairly certain that it would be my thoughtful boyfriend checking up on me.

"Good morning," I said cheerily as I opened the door. We'd

taken the significant step of giving each other house keys, but gentleman that he was, Briggs still always knocked first.

"You look much better." He walked inside and held up a tall white cup. "I've brought you something called a blueberry blast. It's basically a blueberry smoothie with all kinds of healthy stuff blended in. The girl at the smoothie shop said it's the best thing for a cold." He handed it to me. "I know it's not really the weather for smoothies, but I thought it might give you a little immunity boost."

The cup was cold in my fingers and the fruity scent of blueberries wafted up through the wide straw.

"Smells good. I've always thought that if the color blue had a fragrance, it would smell just like blueberries." I took a sip. "Hmm, delicious. I feel more immune already."

He walked to the kitchen and made himself a cup of coffee. "I thought you'd be dressed for work by now."

"Probably would have been showered and dressed by now but there was this whole thing with my dad wanting to get a pet llama." I sat at the table with the delicious smoothie.

He laughed briefly. "And what would your dad do with a pet llama?"

"Why, use it as a golf caddy, of course." I took another sip.

"Of course. Don't know why I didn't think of that."

"I'm also hesitant to get out of these cozy flannel pajamas. Do you think people would take me seriously as a florist if I wore them to work?"

His chuckle nearly made him spill the coffee he'd just poured. "Not sure if they'd take you seriously, but it would definitely get you some publicity. And you know what they say, any publicity is good publicity. Even murder, apparently. I hear people still want tickets to the play, even though there doesn't seem to be a Dorothy."

Kingston was through being ignored. He dropped down off his

cage and marched over to me. He stared up at me with shiny black eyes, trying his best to impersonate a puppy begging for a treat.

"I suppose you're ready for breakfast," I said.

"I'll get it." Briggs hopped up. He went to the refrigerator and took out two hard boiled eggs. Kingston wasted no time flying back to his cage to wait for the eggs.

"Have you heard anything about the case yet?" I asked.

"Nate called this morning with a preliminary report. Nothing too surprising. The victim died from strangulation with a computer cable. She tried to fight off her attacker, which was the reason for the red marks on her fingertips. She died somewhere between five and seven, after dress rehearsal and before the play was supposed to open."

"That sounds pretty much like what I expected. Where are you going to start?"

"Still sorting that out. I'll talk to a few more of the theater group members and see if anything stands out. Are you going to take the day off and rest?"

"No, I'm not that frail, James. I think I can manage a work day with a little cold."

He looked properly chastised. "Sorry, I just worry about you is all."

"I know and it's sweet." I took another sip of the smoothie. "I'm feeling so much better today, I'll probably have enough energy to run a flower shop and solve a murder on the side."

His crooked smile, my personal favorite, appeared. "I have no doubt of that."

CHAPTER 17

Some of the chill in the air and, thankfully, in my bones had disappeared. It was shaping up to be a beautiful morning, and I was feeling better every minute. The blueberry blast might just have done the trick. Ryder had been moping around the store all morning, tending to his tasks without his usual energy.

I thumbed through my bridal bouquet notebooks looking at arrangements with freesias. I was expecting a bridal customer, and she had mentioned that she was leaning toward freesias. Freesias were a wonderful flower that came in a variety of vivid colors and always carried a sweet perfume. They were perfect in vases and bouquets because they lasted a long time. Though she had specified freesias, she never mentioned color.

I decided to take Ryder's mind off of his imminent departure and Lola's subsequent pout with the topic of flowers. "The bride says she wants freesias. There are so many to choose from." I kept talking even though I wasn't entirely sure he was listening. He had busied himself with the dull task of cleaning the potting table. "I think a bridal bouquet would require at least one of the white species like Ballerina or Ambassador," I said. "The white blooms are an elegant way to highlight one of the brighter colored freesia, like Blue Bayou with its violet blue petals and bright yellow center, or, since it is a fall wedding, maybe some dark orange Clementines."

I looked his direction waiting for a response. He wiped the potting counter as if he was shining a prize automobile.

"Ryder, that is just the potting table. It's not going into any showroom."

He glanced up. "Huh?" He looked back at the table. "Right, guess my mind isn't on my work."

"It'll all work out, Ryder. And Lola is happy for you. I spoke to her last night."

"Really?" he asked.

"Sure, you know how she likes a good bit of drama. She'll come around, and I know she'll be just as excited for you as I am."

Ryder looked pointedly at the bridal notebook in front of me. "Except I'm leaving you without an assistant at the worst possible time."

"I'll manage. I'm sure I can find someone to help me in the store."

The bell signaled that my bridal customer had arrived. A young woman, who I'd seen in the store on other occasions, walked in looking just like every other future bride. Rosy cheeked, bright eyed and just a little bit freaked out. Weddings were so much work and stress, I sometimes wondered how the tradition had lasted through so many centuries. Fortunately for us florists, the wedding industry was big and booming as usual. Since the older woman at her side took the time to reach over and adjust a shiny blue barrette in the younger woman's hair, I quickly deduced she was Mom.

"We're here to look at some bridal bouquets. Hopefully, you'll have what we're looking for," the mother said primly. She adjusted her purse on her arm.

I caught the daughter's quick eye roll before she reached her hand forward. "I'm Penny and this is my mother, Wendy. You came highly recommended by my friend Ashley, Ashley Penbroke."

"Oh yes, I remember Ashley." I tapped my chin in thought.

"Cascading orchids and hydrangeas," Ryder said from the other side of the store.

"Yes," Penny said with a wide smile. "You have a good memory," she told him. The little positive moment seemed to put some spring back into his step.

"We don't do cascading orchids too often." Ryder looked at me. "I've got a few bouquets to deliver locally. I'll be back in an hour."

"Great." I turned back to my customers. "I've pulled out the notebooks that contain the freesia bouquets." We walked to the island, and I motioned for them to sit on the stools. "Do you know what your accent color will be? Are you going with autumn colors?"

As I spoke, Wendy squinted at me. "You were with Detective Briggs last night at that terrible disaster of a play."

Penny elbowed her lightly. "Mom, everyone knows that Detective Briggs is dating Pink of Pink's Flowers."

Wendy wriggled to a better posture on her stool. "You know I don't bother myself with town gossip." She turned to me. "Is it true that poor girl was murdered? Do you think they'll still have a play?"

"Mother," Penny said slightly aghast. "How can you worry about that when someone has been killed?"

"Well, excuse me, Penny, but your father and I were looking very forward to that play."

"Yes, it was disappointing," I said calmly to cool off the discussion. I flipped open the notebook. "I assume you'll want some white freesias, or maybe you were thinking of using a second flower."

"I'm thinking white and possibly a blue or lavender," Penny said. "You know it might have been the actor playing Tin Man, or, at the very least, someone who had reason to be jealous of him."

My ears perked up. "Oh, why do you say that?"

"Remember, Mom, when I told you Debbie and I saw the two actors sitting on the bench on the wharf?" Penny turned to me. "It was yesterday afternoon. Late. maybe just before three. The woman was dressed as Dorothy and the man was dressed as the Tin Man. At first she seemed to be angry with him. She pushed away his hand a couple of times but eventually she was smiling and then they looked cozy. Or as cozy as one could get with a Tin Man," she added with a laugh, then her expression changed. "Wow, I guess that was the woman who was murdered. I hadn't thought of that until just now. Gosh, I might have been one of the last people to see her alive." She seemed overly proud of the grim fact but then she was young and probably didn't know too many dead people.

I calculated in my head some of the timeline. It seemed Amanda Seton had had a busy schedule ahead of the three o'clock dress rehearsal. First, she took a trip to Elsie's bakery with Gordon. Then she left him and took a walk on the wharf with Johnny. Both witnesses, Elsie and Penny, described the interactions as flirty and cozy. Instantly, I wondered if the two men knew about the other's off stage *friendship* with the leading lady.

"All right, enough of the gossip, Penny. We need to get serious about picking flowers for this wedding, or you'll have to walk down the aisle holding daisies from my garden."

Penny perked up on the stool. "Exactly right, Mom. Let's go through the notebook."

"I placed a pink tab to show you all the pages that contain bouquets with freesias. These are just sample ideas. You can make any customized changes you like. I'll give you some time to browse the notebook. I'll just be over at the potting table if you need me."

"Thanks," Penny said.

I walked over to the potting area and pulled some mini pots from the shelf. Tom and Gigi had asked for some oregano plants and the nursery had delivered some flats. My mind drifted to the murder case. Gordon was seeing Constance but also spent *quality* time with Amanda. Amanda was also spending time with Johnny. Elsie was right. It seemed as if there was some hanky panky going on in Oz, after all.

CHAPTER 18

The wedding order along with several other special occasion orders took most of the morning. The blueberry blast had run its course, and my stomach was growling. Ryder had taken Lola to a special lunch, hoping to cheer her up. (My friend knew how to use drama to her advantage.)

As if she had some sort of special sixth sense, which would not have been the least bit surprising, Elsie strolled in carrying two bowls that smelled divine and had long tails of steam.

She placed a bowl down. "Lunch to help zap away that cold. I was making Les his *grumble* lunch of quinoa, sweet potatoes and broccoli and I decided to make extra for you."

I lowered my nose to the bowl. "Hmm, garlic and onions. Did you say this is Les's grumble lunch?"

"Yes. Remember I've got him on the healthy diet during the week."

"How can we forget," I said. "He laments his hardship all the time. So I suppose grumble lunch because he grumbles and complains about it so much?"

"You've got it."

"No complaints from me," I said. "I'm hungry so your timing is perfect."

Elsie spun around. "Got to take grumpy man his bowl next."

"You should tell him to come eat with me," I suggested. "Maybe I can lead by example."

Elsie returned with her brother's lunch bowl and placed it next to mine. "Good idea. Text him and invite him to lunch in the flower shop. He'll be happy to come if the invite is from you. And I've got a batch of brownies in the oven."

"I thought I smelled cocoa and butter seeping through the walls. I suppose it would negate all the beneficial qualities of this lunch if I finished it with a fudgy brownie."

"Does sort of defeat the purpose, but I'll bring you one later after grumpy man has left. He's got high cholesterol. You've got a cold. You can still eat a brownie." With that she strode out Elsie style and headed back to the bakery.

I grabbed my phone and sent Les a text. He didn't bother to answer but showed up with a smile and a bright green sweater just two minutes later.

"So she's making you suffer too," he said as he spotted the identical bowls.

Kingston dropped down from his perch and hopped across the floor to greet Les. Les stopped and leaned down to pet his head. "Kingston, how do you feel about broccoli?"

"He would never say no to broccoli, but something tells me your sister would know if you fed it to my bird." I patted the stool next to me. "Sit and we'll get healthy together."

His blue-gray eyes twinkled. "Those vegetables are certainly going to go down a lot smoother with you as my lunch date." He climbed up on the stool. "So, what's new in Lacey's world? Aside from another murder investigation. I heard about Dorothy's death."

"Yes, it wasn't exactly the night at the theater I was envisioning when I talked James into buying tickets."

Les pulled a packet of salt out of his pocket and pressed his finger to his lips. "Don't tell her. I just need a little salt to make this stuff more palatable." He sprinkled some on and offered me a sprinkle. Which I accepted. The cold had made my taste buds dull, and there was nothing like salt to pep them up.

"Have they found the killer?" he asked.

"I'm afraid I've been too busy to get any updates from James, but I don't think this will be solved quickly unless someone steps forward and confesses. But I have moved forward on the Hawksworth mystery. Or, at least, I think I have. It's all still theories, but if my hunches are correct, I think Harvard Price was somehow connected to the whole thing. And our current Mayor Price is not too pleased about me snooping around in his family history, which only makes my theory stronger."

Les picked through the green veggies to the sweet potato chunks. "It's long been known that Price's great grandfather was a shifty character."

I nearly choked on my quinoa. (Not easy to do.) "Is that right? How do you know that? Why is this the first time I'm hearing it?"

Les shrugged. "I had no idea you were connecting Harvard Price to the Hawksworth murders. Otherwise, I would have told you all about his shady dealings. There were even rumors about him cheating his way into the mayor's office."

I just about slipped off my stool. "Really? How do you know all this about Harvard?"

"George, one of the guys I go bowling with on Saturday nights, had a great uncle who lived to be ninety-nine. The uncle worked as a fisherman on some salty old captain's boat. That captain had a particular disliking for Fielding Price, Harvard's son and Harlan's grandfather. Apparently, Fielding lost big in a poker game to the captain but he refused to pay up. Even threatened to use his mayoral power to revoke the guy's fishing license. Anyhow, that captain told George's uncle all kinds of tales about cheating and scandals and how the Prices always bought their way into the mayor's office." He picked through to the next sweet potato.

"Maybe if you couple that sweet potato with the piece of broccoli it won't taste so *green*," I suggested.

He rocked his head side to side considering my proposal, then dove in for the next sweet potato.

"Should I take George's uncle's Price gossip"—I pointed to the empty salt packet—"You know—with a grain of salt? After all, it seems that sea captain had good reason to start some tall tales about the Price family."

Les was out of sweet potato, so he put his fork down. "George wasn't the first person who mentioned that Harvard Price was a shifty politician. I've heard other people say it. I'm just too old to remember who. I think some of the guys in the firehouse used to talk about our mayor, then gossip about his predecessors always popped up. From what I remember, Harlan's dad, Denton Price, was likable. I don't think he was up to anything shady. He won because he was polite and willing to listen to people."

I stabbed a piece of broccoli. "Too bad his son didn't inherit any of those qualities."

Les looked up from his disappointing lunch. "Is that old grump giving you trouble again?"

"Let's just say he wasn't too pleased to find me in his office poring over old obituaries."

He chuckled until he realized I was serious. "Why were you looking at obituaries in his office?"

I sat forward, eager to tell him all I knew. "I was searching for information about a baby girl who died just shortly after birth in 1906. Her mother, Jane Price, Harvard's daughter from his first marriage, died in childbirth, and her sickly baby was sent to live with the father. I think Bertram Hawksworth was the father." I squeezed his arm. "But don't say a word to George or your bowling buddies or anyone, for that matter. I've been warned by a certain detective not to get ahead of myself on this. I need solid proof before I can determine whether or not my theory holds water."

"No kidding? Well, that might just have been enough to send Harvard into a rage. Maybe enough to kill Hawksworth." He pushed the mostly full bowl away like a kid at the dinner table signaling he was done and there was nothing his mom could say to make him clean his plate. The poor guy really wasn't a fan of vegetables. "But seems sort of drastic to kill the whole Hawksworth family, don't you think?"

"I do but I'll figure it out. Just wait and see."

He laughed. "Then the mayor won't just try and run your bird out of town. He'll try to send you packing with him."

"You're probably right, but a murder investigator has to put her own needs aside to find the killer."

Les looked down at his unfinished bowl. "How does a murder investigator feel about keeping this lunch secret? I can't sit through another sisterly lecture about wasting food."

"I feel slightly traitorous keeping secrets from Elsie, but as far as I'm concerned you ate vegetables. After all, sweet potato counts as a veggie."

"Thank goodness for sweet potatoes."

CHAPTER 19

*R*yder had come back from his special lunch with Lola considerably cheerier than the morning. And I was feeling back to my old self again. Thank goodness it was a short cold and not some long, drawn out flu. We'd hit the usual afternoon lull in the shop, so I used it as my chance to do some investigating.

The usual flutter of activity at the town square had slowed considerably. Group members were meandering around the square in pairs and threes, likely a safety precaution. Despite the sunny skies, there was a general cloud of gloom over the whole scene. What was noticeably absent was the sense of invigorated purpose I'd noticed the day before. Yesterday, people had tasks, whether it was painting a prop tree or sitting under a real tree studying lines with a partner, everyone had something to do with one common goal in mind—putting on a stellar opening night performance. This afternoon, the frenetic creativity and anticipation had been replaced by sorrow, angst and, I could only assume, mistrust. It was entirely likely that someone they had been traveling, living and working with for months or even years was a cold-blooded killer. That would definitely dampen team spirit and cooperation.

The day before, I could never have walked freely through the area, but today, everyone was in their own heads, too steeped in their own thoughts and worries to care about a lone woman strolling along the path. No one paid me much attention as I pretended to look at the scenery while eavesdropping on conversations. One particularly loud one was happening next to the tent. Three crew members were touching up paint on a large wooden cutout of Emerald City. It was an impressive piece sitting on a dozen or so wheels for easy movement. Their backs were toward me as they focused on their task of touching up the green paint.

"If you ask me, she just pushed too hard for all her special treatment," a woman said to the man next to her. "I don't know why she thought she deserved spa days and fancy flavored coffees. We all worked just as hard as her. Someone must have finally gotten sick and tired of her constant complaining and whining."

The guy lowered his brush and looked at the woman. "Do you think it was Susie?" he asked point blank. His gaze flitted to the nosy woman lingering behind them. He elbowed the woman and whispered something in her ear. She took a not too subtle look over her shoulder. I moved along without the answer on whether or not the woman with the green paintbrush thought Susana Damon was the culprit.

Five or six people, Johnny included, were eating lunch on one of the picnic tables in the square. The group chatted and there was even an occasional laugh. From my vantage point, it seemed that Johnny was quite the entertainer. He spoke animatedly about something and his audience chuckled. It was an oddly cheery scene considering what had transpired the night before. It seemed not everyone was broken up about Amanda's death. From the conversation I overheard just a moment earlier, it almost seemed as if some people thought Amanda brought her demise on herself with so many demands and expectations to be treated better than everyone else.

I spotted Constance walking across the grass to Susana's trailer. She walked up the steps, knocked and entered seconds later. I hurried across the path and grass to the backside of Susana's trailer. It was a sunny day. With any luck, a window would be open so I could hear their conversation. Susana had a noticeably loud, clear voice, an attribute suited for her job. I could hear her before I even reached the trailer. I scooted around to the backside and stood quietly beneath the tiny open window that, according to my calculations, was right over the kitchen sink.

"We can't afford to refund the tickets, Susie. We should just move opening night to Sunday." Constance's tone was much more muted than Susana's, but I could hear it perfectly through the open window. I kept an eye out for people passing by. I didn't want to be caught eavesdropping. Most people saw me with Detective Briggs. He even introduced me several times as his assistant. I didn't want people to be suspicious about how the case was being run.

"It doesn't seem right," Susie said. "Our lead actress is dead. Murdered right on our stage."

"Yes, I know and I understand your apprehension, but how can we afford to stay open if we have to return all the tickets? Cast members and stage crew will expect to be paid. I know all of Dorothy's lines. Let me play Dorothy. As they say in our business, the show must go on."

I turned my ear up to listen for Susana's answer, but voices were nearing the trailer. I reluctantly left the spot below the window and wandered casually back into the town square.

I spotted two young women walking away from the trailers and heading toward the wharf. They looked friendly and, with any luck, chatty. Maybe it was time to come out of the eavesdropping shadows and talk to a few of the group members face to face.

CHAPTER 20

I strolled casually behind my two targets. They were both young, early twenties. One was under five feet and petite. She was wearing an old, nicely timeworn bomber jacket that was a few sizes too big and landed nearly at her knees. I quickly determined the unusual piece of attire would be the perfect conversation starter. Her friend was just a smidge taller with bleached white hair and long bangs. Neither of them looked too distraught about what had happened. They chatted amiably as they headed toward the hot dog stand. There was a long line, so I got in behind them. I wasn't in need of any lunch, but the stand also sold delicious lemonade.

"Do you think Constance will convince Susie to open the show?" one woman asked the other as they stood in front of me.

"I hope so. We're all anxious to see the play," I said, interjecting myself into their conversation with a polite smile.

They looked back at me apprehensively as if it had been something they didn't want overheard. I decided to change tactics and hop back to my original plan. I pointed to the bomber jacket.

"This is the greatest jacket. It looks like the real thing. Not one of those fakes they sell at the mall."

The woman's lips turned up in a proud smile as she smoothed her hand over the supple, worn leather. "It is original. It belonged to my grandfather. It took me some pretty heavy duty begging, but he finally let me have it."

"It's amazing," I said.

Her friend squinted at me. "Aren't you the woman who was with the detective last night?"

"Yes," I said. It wasn't the turn in conversation I was hoping for, but I decided it could work to my advantage. I stuck out my hand. "I'm Lacey. How do you do?"

"I'm Joan," the woman in the bomber jacket said. "And this is Carly. We're with the cast."

"I thought you two looked like actors. Something in the animated way you two were speaking to each other." The line moved closer to the order window. "By the way, I highly recommend the chili dog. The chili is tasty."

"That's what I was planning on ordering," Joan said.

Carly looked at her. "I thought you were getting the sauerkraut dog."

Joan shrugged but it was hardly noticeable in the oversized jacket. "I think the sauerkraut might mess with my stomach."

"Well, a chili dog isn't exactly like sipping warm milk," Carly noted. I hadn't planned to start a hot dog debate with my suggestion. I was only four hot dog customers away from losing them to the order window. I needed to keep the conversation moving now that we'd become acquainted.

"What parts do you two play?" I asked. I had a sneaking suspicion due to their diminutive size.

"We're members of the Lollipop Guild," Joan said happily. "You probably could have guessed that."

I smiled. "I didn't want to assume. Excuse me, but I overheard you two talking about the possibility of reopening the play again."

They exchanged cautious looks trying to decide if they should say anything, then Joan shrugged again. "We can't really afford to travel all this way and set up camp and tents and props and not put on a play. Refunding tickets could drain funds. We really need to do the shows."

"I see. That makes sense. It was terribly tragic. I'm sure it will be hard for all of you to put on a performance when one of your close friends is dead. And, on top of it, she was the star of the play."

"Yeah, we're all broken up about it, of course. It was a big shock," Joan said.

"And scary too," Carly said with a visible shudder. "Someone we know might be a killer."

"Yes, I'm sure that has you all worried," I said. "Who do you think might have disliked the actress enough to kill her?"

They both took furtive glances around, apparently checking to see who was nearby, before scooting closer. "I don't like talking bad about the dead, but Amanda was sort of a diva," Joan said in a hushed tone. "She was sure that the play couldn't go on without her. She considered herself irreplaceable, and she let everyone know it. Most of us just avoided her because she wasn't fun to be around," Joan said.

"Unless you were one of the many men in the cast," Carly added cattily.

"Oh? So Amanda was seeing some of the cast members?" We moved up another customer closer to the order window.

"Who knows?" Joan scoffed. "It was hard to keep up with all her different relationships. Let's just say she bounced around between boyfriends and that didn't win her any friends either. Amanda liked to be the center of attention, whether on stage or off."

The person at the window only ordered a lemonade, so we moved up again and it was Joan and Carly's turn to order.

I made a show of glancing at my phone. "Oh wow, I didn't realize how late it was. Guess I'll have to skip the hot dog. Enjoy your lunch. It was nice talking to you."

"Bye, nice talking to you," Joan said as I broke away from the line.

It wasn't just a ruse. I really did need to head back to the shop. I'd been away too long. I took a short cut through the town square and was gifted with one more bit of knowledge, aside from the nuggets I'd gleamed from Joan and Carly.

Constance had apparently finished her conversation with Susana. She was sitting on a bench near the fountain. Gordon was sitting next to her with his arm around her shoulder. I caught a flirtatious smile before Constance rested her head against him. It seemed they were back on solid footing as a couple. Or maybe they had never been off of it. Elsie had made the observation that Dorothy and Scarecrow, Amanda and Gordon, had been amorous during their visit to the bakery, but maybe Elsie had misread the scene. Although, that was highly unlikely. Elsie was very observant. I couldn't really remember the last time she was wrong about something. And Constance was definitely acting distracted and upset when I ran into her at the pharmacy. It would have been easy to think she'd discovered Amanda and Gordon together with the way she was acting.

Whether or not Amanda and Gordon had been flirting or whether or not they'd been caught, it seemed Constance and Gordon were a happy couple again now that Dorothy was out of the picture for good.

CHAPTER 21

The late afternoon sun cast a warm glow through the front window of the shop, and a golden light flowed down the short hallway and into my office. I gazed absently at my order pad as my fingers fluttered away filling in the numbers on my last purchase order. Of all the tasks in the flower shop, paperwork was by far my least favorite. At least I didn't have to write grueling, detailed reports like Briggs. And then, as if my thought had conjured him, the bell rang. Seconds later, Briggs poked his head into the office. The afternoon glow seeping down the hallway illuminated his handsome face. His brown eyes were like dark cocoa, and his hair was back to its naturally disheveled state.

"Am I interrupting?" he asked.

I finished the final entry and patted my stack of orders. "Nope. Your timing is perfect. I was just about to doze right off onto my keyboard. Why is paperwork so boring?"

He stepped into the office. "I'd take your paperwork over mine any day."

"No, thanks. I could never be a detective if part of the job description was writing reports. I'll stick to investigating on the side. No paperwork involved. Which reminds me—" I started but the front bell rang.

"Ryder was just heading out as I walked inside. He told me to tell you," Briggs said.

"I guess I need to get out there. Where was he going?"

"He was carrying a nice bouquet. I think he was heading across the street to Lola's."

I stood up from my desk and tilted my head side to side to take the kink out of my neck. "That poor guy is going to drive himself crazy until he leaves. Then he'll probably drive himself more crazy when he's halfway around the world."

"He's leaving?" Briggs asked as he followed me into the hallway. We both stopped our conversation when we saw that my next customer wasn't a customer at all.

Mayor Price was standing a good distance away from Kingston's perch. His angry eyes were set deep in his round face as he glowered at the bird. Kingston was eyeing him rather suspiciously too. My bird had a sixth sense when it came to people.

Mayor Price saw me first and hadn't noticed Briggs yet. "Miss Pinkerton." He wasted no time with greetings or niceties. (Not that I was expecting any.) "I've come here to let you know that I don't appreciate you digging up old history about this town or, in particular, my family." His face grew redder as he spoke. He opened his mouth to continue but sputtered and sucked back in the words when Briggs stepped into the front room.

"Briggs"—he finally found his tongue—"You need to tell this woman—" He added a rude, pointing finger in case Briggs didn't know *which* woman he was referring to.

Briggs walked forward with his own gesture. His hand was up telling him to stop. "Hold on there, Mayor Price. You haven't finished your statement, but I already don't like your tone. You may call her Miss Pinkerton. And I don't *tell* her anything. She's an independent woman who makes up her own mind."

"Briggs, she's been sticking her nose into places it doesn't belong. I know she helps you occasionally because of some perceived extraordinary sense of smell." A slight eye roll followed. "But she has no business drudging up things about my family's past."

"First of all"—Briggs had lowered his hand and his voice—"Her hyperosmia is not *perceived*. It exists. She can detect miniscule odors that our evidence team would never smell, and she has helped solve numerous cases with her nose. And secondly, she has every right to research the history of this town. It just so happens your family has been a big part of Port Danby for many years. There is no way to separate one from the other."

Mayor Price stepped forward in a menacing fashion but quickly remembered he was staring down an opponent who didn't scare easily. Briggs kept a calm demeanor, but his shoulders were taut and that little twitchy muscle in his jaw flickered beneath the dark beard stubble.

"She may research all she wants, but she needs to stay clear of the Price name." The mayor threatened.

I'd stood back like a meek kitten for long enough. "You certainly are worried that I'll dig up something unbecoming about your family," I said briskly.

Briggs shot me a side eyed 'thanks for making things worse' look. "Lacey is not digging into the Price family history. She is simply trying to figure out what happened to the Hawksworth family. The evidence doesn't match up to a murder suicide. It seems right that after all these years, someone takes the time to clear Bertram Hawksworth's name if he was a victim and not a killer. She might even find that he actually did it but—"

Mayor Price swung his thick arm around fast enough to startle Kingston. The bird stayed on his perch but flapped his long black wings. The mayor instantly ducked and curled his arms around his face. "Don't let that bird near me."

That was when something dawned on me and, suddenly, things made sense. The mayor was afraid of crows. From his reaction, I could only deduce that he'd had, at some point in time, a frightful encounter with a crow or maybe even a flock of crows.

"You just startled him. He won't hurt you." I immediately rushed over to Kingston's treat can and pulled out a snack to calm him, giving him something else to focus on other than the scary man with the angry tone.

Mayor Price reluctantly lowered his arms and scowled at Kingston. "Wild animals have no place inside a store," he barked.

"I think we've already done the rounds on that particular topic," Briggs said wryly. "And I think the other topic too. If you can't produce any law or ordinance that bars a Port Danby citizen from researching the town's history, you have no legal right or right of any kind to stop Lacey from investigating the Hawksworth murders."

Price's double chin billowed out with a mean laugh. "Waste of time anyhow. The case was solved back when it happened. She's just chasing myths and fantasies. Maybe she should find something better to do with her time."

"You mean like run a successful Port Danby business?" I chirruped with an overly sweet smile.

Briggs crossed his arms as a gesture to let him know I'd had the last word, and we were done with the conversation.

With his impeccable timing, Kingston had finished his treat. He swooped off his perch and headed toward the work island. Price nearly fell backward over his own big feet in his attempt to flee the shop. He slammed out so hard, the goat bell that had hung there for two years, clattered and clanged as it bounced along the tile floor.

Briggs walked over to pick up the fallen bell.

"Argh, that man is aggravating," I said. I hadn't realized I was shaking about the whole thing until I reached up to push a curl off my face. My fingers were trembling. Briggs noticed and walked over with one of his calming smiles.

He took my hand between his, and instantly, the trembling stopped. "Don't let him get to you. He takes his position of mayor far too seriously, as if he is some kind of king or something." He saw that I was still slightly shaken, so he did exactly what I was hoping he would do. He put his strong arms around me and held me close.

I rested my cheek against his shoulder. "It's strange, isn't it? How obsessed he is with me searching into his family history."

Briggs' deep voice rumbled against my cheek as he spoke. "I'd say you've definitely stepped on a nerve. He must know about some of the skeletons in his family closet. They must be embarrassing or scandalous enough that he doesn't want them to surface."

I peered up at him. "You mean scandalous like a daughter having an illegitimate baby?" I sighed. "Even when I say it with a touch of drama, it doesn't sound nearly bad enough to murder an entire family. By the way, thank you for handling that so well, and thank you for reminding him I'm an independent woman." I rested against him again. "An independent woman who depends on these strong, comforting arms every once in awhile."

"And there's no one these arms would rather comfort than you."

CHAPTER 22

*R*yder returned from delivering flowers to Lola. I was still feeling out of sorts from the mayor's visit, so Briggs suggested a short walk. The sun was setting and the temperature was dropping, but the cool air felt refreshing. We decided not to discuss Mayor Price at all on the walk, but I broke the promise in the first few steps.

"I know we weren't going to bring up that grumpy man, but I just need to ask you one thing. Did you notice his extreme reaction to King flapping his wings? I've seen people startle when Kingston stretched his wings or flew down from his perch, but I've never seen anyone take cover like Mayor Price."

"I thought the same thing. That might be why he wanted Kingston banned from being in the store. Maybe Price had a bad experience with a crow."

"Ah ha, so you were thinking the same thing as me." I nodded sharply. "There—last mention of *that* man." A fog was drifting in, so, for a change, we strolled away from the coast. "We never had a chance to discuss the Oz case." Just as I said it his phone rang.

He pulled it out. "That's forensics. They were working on

unlocking Amanda's phone." He answered it. "Briggs here." I could hear the voice but not the clear words of the person on the other end. We stopped in front of the Mod Frock so Briggs could finish his call. I took a few minutes to admire a cute, yellow sundress, the owner, Kate Yardley, had placed on a mannequin. It would be perfect for summer.

"Just learned something interesting," Briggs said as he hung up. "Remember that Susana said she left Amanda in the tent after their little meeting. I think I know why she stuck around. There was a text on Amanda's phone. It was from Gordon. He asked her if they could meet up after dress rehearsal. She wrote back that she had a meeting with Susana first and that she'd wait for him in the tent."

I stopped and my mouth dropped open. "Whoa, that's not just something interesting. That's huge. But then, would he seriously be stupid enough to text Amanda to meet him there if he was planning to kill her? And what would his motive be?"

"Both good questions. Looks like I'm going to need to talk to him. Do you think you can extend the walk?"

"Sure. Let's go by the shop. I'll tell Ryder he can close up early. We're slow this afternoon. Then I can fill you in on some of the things I learned when I snooped around the theater camp today."

"Why am I not surprised about that," he said.

We stopped at the flower shop. I dashed in to grab my keys and my coat. I let Ryder know he could lock up early, then Briggs and I headed toward the foggy coast. I buttoned up my coat.

"Why always fog? Couldn't we just have a nice breezy evening for a change? So do you think it was Gordon?"

A short laugh followed. "We're a little short on evidence for that, but the text messages are not good for Gordon. However, it's hard to get a conviction on just a few texts. We'll need more. And like you said earlier, what would his motive be?"

"Well, I might have something," I said. "This afternoon when I snooped around at the theater site, I overheard—"

Briggs nodded. "Good word for it."

"Yes, one can't help it if words float to their ears, can they? Anyhow, a few of the crew members were talking about how Amanda was always too demanding, always wanting special treatment. I didn't get any vibes that they were fond of her. In fact, when I started up a conversation with two eager to talk cast members, I got the distinct impression that she wasn't too well liked. With the exception of several of the men. It seemed Amanda liked to flirt and start up relationships with some of the male cast members. They said she bounced from boyfriend to boyfriend. It sounded as if there was much to gossip about in the troupe."

"Behavior like that does occasionally cause jealousy and crimes of passion. Did they give any specific names?" Briggs asked.

"No names but there was Elsie's observation that Dorothy and the Scarecrow seemed pretty flirty. Then a bridal customer told me she saw Dorothy and the Tin Man cozied up on a bench on the wharf. Maybe Gordon found out she wasn't faithful, and he was jealous enough to kill her."

"Could be as simple as that," Briggs admitted. "The text messages sure put him in the center of things."

We stopped in front of Franki's to breathe in the warm scent of her spicy chili. "We need to make time for a chili and cornbread dinner," I said.

"I wouldn't say no to that." We continued on. "Did you find out anything else of interest when you snooped around the site?"

I rubbed my chin. "Hmm, let me see. Oh yes, how could I forget. I mean I had to do some considerable sneaking. I saw Constance, the woman who I mentioned was Gordon's supposed longtime girlfriend—although, those lines are sort of blurred now, I guess. Anyhow, she walked into Susana's trailer, so I took the liberty of sneaking around the back of the trailer and hunching down below an open window to—" I cleared my throat, "to overhear their conversation."

Briggs reached around and squeezed me closer. "I'm pretty sure what you just described to me surpasses the definition of over-hearing, but continue."

"During their conversation, Constance was trying to convince Susana to open the show back up. She said they couldn't afford to refund all the tickets."

"Makes sense," Briggs said. We were just turning the corner. The full scale of the traveling theater caravan loomed into view. "It must cost a fortune to travel from town to town with all these trucks and trailers."

"Not to mention labor and costumes and salaries for the cast," I added.

"Right but how do you put on *The Wizard of Oz* without Dorothy?" Briggs asked.

"From what I picked up during my little *overhearing* session, Constance, who normally plays a Munchkin and a flying monkey, reminded Susana that she knew all of Dorothy's lines. Makes sense. I always thought there was an understudy for characters with a big part. Constance could, apparently, step in to take Amanda's place. When I think about it, Constance is a much better match for the iconic Garland Dorothy. She's petite with large round eyes. I'm surprised she wasn't cast for the part in the first place."

"Did Susana agree?" Briggs asked. "I'm asking less for the case and more for whether or not I have to get out my theater clothes again."

I laughed lightly and took his arm. "I heard voices and chickened out. I didn't want to get caught snooping under the window. "

"Probably good thinking. I guess we'll find out soon enough if the show goes on, as they say. But now, let's find that darn Scarecrow."

CHAPTER 23

*I*t just so happened that the first people we stumbled upon were Joan and Carly. They had pulled yoga mats out onto a flat section of grass, and they were just finishing what looked like a meditation session. "These are the girls who gave me the scoop about Amanda hopping from boyfriend to boyfriend. The smaller one is named Joan, and she has a very cool old bomber jacket she begged off her grandfather."

"Does the jacket have anything to do with the case?" he asked wryly.

"Nope, just making a general comment about the cool jacket."

Carly peered up through her long bangs and elbowed her friend, who was still sitting with eyes closed and hands in the prayer position.

Joan opened her eyes and scowled at Carly for disrupting her meditation. Carly muttered something to her. It was easy enough to figure out what she'd said.

"Lacey," Joan said politely. "Nice to see you again. Hello, Detective," she said with a noticeable bat of her lashes. She hopped up to her tiny feet. "Have you found the person who killed Amanda? I sure hope it's no one we know. I was just telling Carly before we started our yoga session that I would rather we found out some drifter or crazy person just happened through town and decided to kill someone. That way we wouldn't find out that we've been living with a killer, and we wouldn't lose any more people from the troupe."

"Of course, understandable," I said, not entirely sure how to respond to her logic. If some random mad killer was on the loose, it would be even more dangerous than if someone had a motive and reason to kill Amanda. "Have either of you seen Gordon Houser?" I asked, sensing that Briggs was ready to move on from Joan and Carly.

"Not recently," Joan said. She did a quick scan of the area. "His blond hair is usually easy to spot, like a brightly colored car in a parking lot," she added with a laugh. She crinkled her nose up at us. "Why do you need to talk to Gordon?"

Knowing already that they both liked to gossip about their fellow cast members, I answered briefly. "We just need a few details from him. Nothing important."

Carly pushed to her feet. "Oh wait, I think I heard him telling someone that he was going for a run on the beach before it got too dark. You might find him there."

"Great," Briggs said. "Thanks so much." We headed back toward Pickford Way, figuring we weren't going to be able to avoid a walk on the moist sand, but we never even reached the wharf.

It was easy enough to spot Gordon Houser. He was jogging, with his usual heavy-footed gait, along the sidewalk on Pickford Way. He had on dark sunglasses and a sweatband circled his head. His straw yellow hair stuck out in every direction. His running shoes were coated in sand.

He hadn't noticed Briggs and I were the couple walking toward him until Briggs said hello. His chest heaved with breaths as he stopped to find out who was addressing him. He took off his sunglasses.

"Detective Briggs, did you need to see me? I was running on the beach," he added quickly, making it sound defensive.

Briggs looked pointedly at his large shoes. "Yes, I can see that. Hope you had a good run. I just needed to talk to you about something." Briggs pulled out his notepad and read from it. "You sent Amanda Seton a text at 3:30 P.M. on Thursday asking her to stay in the tent after dress rehearsal so you two could meet up."

He blinked at Briggs for a long moment. "No I didn't. I never asked her to stay after dress rehearsal." He shifted uncomfortably on his big feet. "Who told you that? What's this all about? I never sent her a text."

Briggs spoke calmly to keep Gordon from growing more agitated. "So you didn't send Amanda a text on Thursday at 3:30?"

"Absolutely not. Whoever told you that is lying. In fact, I'd like to know who told you that. They're obviously trying to frame me. You're looking at the wrong person. I had no reason to kill Amanda. We got along great." He seemed to be genuinely puzzled and irate about the accusation.

"Mr. Houser, in our evidence search, we gained possession of Miss Seton's phone. There was a short text exchange between the two of you. You asked her to meet you in the tent after dress rehearsal to which she replied that she had a meeting with Susana first and that she'd meet you after."

"None of this is true," Gordon countered emphatically.

"So you didn't meet Amanda in the tent after rehearsal?" Briggs prodded.

"No, like I told you last night, after rehearsal, I went to my trailer for a few shots of whiskey. I fell asleep. That's all. I never saw Amanda after rehearsal."

"Then you wouldn't mind if we looked at your phone," Briggs suggested.

"Not at all. I keep it with me at all times." He reached into the pocket of his running shorts and produced the phone. His fingers tiptoed over the screen to unlock it. He swiped over to his contact list and tapped on Amanda. His blond brows bunched thickly below deep lines of confusion. "I didn't send these texts." The ruddiness from the run on the beach faded instantly. He looked up with an expression that bordered on terrified. "I swear I did not send these texts." His face suddenly lit up some. "In fact, I can prove it. I have an alibi. I was on stage at 3:30. We were in the middle of dress rehearsal and I was on stage."

His excuse seemed entirely plausible after hearing Susana's schedule of the afternoon. A main character like Scarecrow would be on stage a lot. He clutched his phone as if he couldn't believe what he was looking at. A few pieces of glitter transferred from his phone to his hand, or it could have been the other way around knowing the *clingy* nature of glitter.

"Looks like your phone picked up some glitter," I noted.

Briggs looked up from his notepad. "Any idea how it got there?"

Gordon was in such a flabbergasted state he couldn't answer right away. He stared at the shiny silver speck on his hand as if it was some strange and unusual thing. "I don't know," he said. There was a touch of surrender in his tone, then he snapped out of his confusion. "I mean the stuff is everywhere. I found a piece on my toast this morning. Some of us have complained to wardrobe telling them the glitter is a catastrophe, but it's already on the Munchkin costumes. Even if we changed those costumes, it seems like we'd never be rid of the glitter."

Briggs moved on from the glitter topic. "Mr. Houser, you said you keep your phone with you at all times."

"Well, yes, in case my agent calls. You don't think I want to stay in this traveling drama group forever, do you? I'm an actor. I'm just waiting for my big break."

"Then was your phone on you during the rehearsal?" Briggs asked.

"No, of course not. Wouldn't be very professional to have your phone ring while you're delivering your lines. I left it in my trailer during dress rehearsal." That revelation seemed to ease his mind. "Obviously someone snuck inside my trailer and sent the text. Not sure why. Now, if that's all, I need to get in and take a shower."

"I don't want to take your phone," Briggs said, "but I might be sending someone over to lift some fingerprints off of it."

Gordon looked somewhat aghast at the prospect. "This phone is covered with my fingerprints. Would you really be able to find someone else's in between all of mine?"

"Probably wouldn't be easy but it couldn't hurt to try."

Gordon looked apprehensive then nodded. "Yeah, I guess if it helps you find out who tried to frame me then that's fine."

Briggs cleared his throat. "Well, the goal is to find the person who killed Amanda Seton. If we find the person who is trying to frame you, that'll be a bonus. But that gives me a question. Do you know of anybody who wanted to see Amanda dead and hurt you in the process?"

He shook his head. "Some of the extras are a little jealous of those of us with starring roles, but I can't think of anyone who is mad enough to commit murder. None of this makes sense. I hope you catch the person soon."

"We will," Briggs said.

Gordon pushed his sunglasses back over his eyes and walked with long, heavy steps toward the trailers.

"Everything he said sounded honest and reasonable," I said. "He looked genuinely baffled and horrified by the texts on his phone."

"True, but don't forget. He's an actor."

CHAPTER 24

*B*riggs decided to stop in and see Susana to find out just what was going on with the play and the group. It gave me an opportunity to chat with Constance. She happened to be helping several of the prop crew with some paint. It seemed they were repairing the damage on the house cutout that fell on Amanda. It was never fully determined how the house fell on her, but Briggs thought it had been pushed down onto her dead body. Amanda had died from strangulation, so the house falling on top of her had no bearing on her death. I wondered if it had been purely symbolic, that, perhaps, Amanda's attacker had considered her to be wicked, like the witch in the story.

I stood back and watched for a second. No one seemed to mind. Constance nodded politely but returned to her task. She lifted a paintbrush to smooth some gray paint on a shingle. The sleeve of the shirt she was wearing dropped back, exposing her arm.

"Oh, your rash is nearly gone," I said. "You must have found the right ointment."

Even though she was grumpy and disgruntled when I ran into

her in the drug store, she was much happier now. She put the brush down and walked over to show me just how improved her skin was.

"It really worked fast too." She lifted her arm for closer inspection.

I pulled away for an unexpected sneeze. "Excuse me. That just came out of nowhere."

"Bless you."

I turned back to her and sneezed again. It was the ointment. It had the same irritant that caused me to sneeze during my nasal inspection of Amanda.

Constance now had my undivided attention. My gaze flashed toward Susana's trailer, but there was no sign of Briggs yet.

"I think there's something in your ointment that makes me sneeze. May I?" I asked pointing to her arm.

Her nicely trimmed brows arched over her big eyes. "Sure, I guess." She lifted her arm again.

I managed to take a long enough whiff to figure out the scent before a small barrage of sneezes took over. Constance covered her mouth in shock. "Wow, are you all right? I guess you're either allergic to me or to the ointment," she said with a laugh.

"I think it's the ointment." I'd learned long ago with a nose like mine to always have a tissue at the ready. I fished deep into my pants pocket and pulled one out. I settled my nose down out of its allergic fit but took a few discrete steps back just to be safe. I should have known earlier what the annoying scent was because I'd always been allergic to it. "By any chance does the ointment have eucalyptus?"

"How did you know?" Constance's cheeks rounded. She was much cheerier than the first few times I met her, the first when she was pleading for roses and the second when she was picking out the ointment. It wouldn't seem odd except that things had not exactly gone swimmingly for the theater troupe these past twenty-four hours. Or maybe she was extra cheery because the person she despised, the woman who was flirting with her longtime boyfriend, was dead.

I wasn't about to start accusing her or asking questions that might put her on defense. "This is going to sound strange," I started, "but, by any chance, did you lend your ointment out to another cast member?"

"You knew that too?" she asked. "It's like you're psychic or something. Tracy and Pete are flying monkeys. They were developing the same rash. We've complained to the makeup and costume team and even to Susana, but they keep telling us it's not in the budget to change things right now. And with Thursday night's cancellation, I'm sure we can just stop thinking about it. We'll be over budget for sure."

"Did the ointment work on their rashes too?" I asked.

"I think so. I haven't asked."

"What's the name of it?" I showed her my hands. "Working in the flower shop gives me rough, dry hands."

She squinted her large eyes in thought. "I think it's called Miracle Salve. It comes in an orange box."

"It sounds like they named the product well. But you only lent it to Tracy and Pete?" I asked. It seemed I was going to have to be more direct.

She looked taken aback by my question. "Yes, I think so." She tilted her head. "Why do you ask?"

"Oh nothing. It's just that, as you may or may not know, I was assisting Detective Briggs with the tragic scene inside the tent." I decided to avoid the phrase murder scene since there were so many people nearby. "I have a very sensitive nose." I tapped it. "As I have no doubt demonstrated by sneezing like crazy. I sneezed last night too, when I got close to Amanda's skin."

Her face froze like stone, and she blended in with the gray shingles behind her. Her reaction might very well have been caused by me bringing up Amanda's skin. Few people like to hear about dead people in detail.

"I think she was using the same ointment," I said.

Her mouth popped into an O and some color returned. "Yes, you're right. You really do have a great nose. I lent Amanda some ointment too. She said the stage makeup was giving her a rash. We keep complaining to Susana that they need to buy better makeup. The stuff they use is cheap."

I'd been so intensely focused on the conversation with Constance, I hadn't noticed Briggs walk up next to me. He cleared his throat to get my attention and let me know he wanted in on the chat.

"Detective Briggs, this is Constance. She plays the part of a Munchkin and a flying monkey," I said politely. He already knew the pertinent details about Constance being Gordon's girlfriend and that she was the actress pleading with Susana to put on the show with Constance standing in as Dorothy.

"How do you do?" Briggs asked. "I thought I heard the name Amanda being mentioned."

Constance piped right up. "I was just explaining to Lacey that I'd lent some of my skin ointment to Amanda because the stage makeup was giving her a rash. It has eucalyptus in it, and it works great on rashes."

I glanced over at Briggs. "Yes, eucalyptus is one of the substances that makes me sneeze."

"Oh, I see," Briggs said with a nod. "So you offered some of the salve on the day of the dress rehearsal and opening night?" he asked.

She nodded. "Sure did." She giggled lightly. "I've lent out the tube so much, I'm going to have to go back to the drug store and buy more." Her friendly smile faded. "Detective Briggs, have you found out who killed Amanda? I saw you going into Susie's trailer, so I thought you might have discovered the name. I sure hope it's no one I know well."

"No killer yet," he said. "But soon." He motioned with his head. "We should be heading back."

"Yes, nice talking to you, Constance," I said before we turned and started back to town.

My phone buzzed as we reached the sidewalk. I pulled it out and read the text from Elsie. "I'm bringing some chocolate croissants to girls' night. Be there at seven."

"Girls' night," I said out loud. "How could I have forgotten about girls' night. We've had this planned for two weeks."

"I take it that means dinner with me is out," Briggs said sounding cutely disappointed.

I grabbed hold of his arm and squeezed it tightly. "I'm sorry about that. Elsie, Lola and I made plans two weeks ago to pig out in comfy clothes and watch Nicholas Sparks movies."

"Nicholas Sparks?" he asked.

I sighed. "You're such a guy."

"Guilty as charged. Now, back to that last conversation. Would someone put ointment on before they were about to be covered in stage makeup? Wouldn't that make the makeup smear?"

I leaned back to give him a shocked looked. "Maybe you're not such a guy, after all. Yes, it does seem odd that someone would put oily salve on before makeup, but I only smelled it faintly on Amanda. In fact, when I moved away from the one spot that made me sneeze I was able to control my allergic reaction. It's possible she used it a few hours before her call to the makeup trailer, and the cream was already well absorbed into her skin. I have to say, I asked Constance several times if she lent the ointment to any other crew members, and she listed off a few but didn't mention Amanda."

That statement slowed his pace. "Interesting. Then how did it come out that she had given some to Amanda?"

I released his arm and pulled my coat tighter. The temperature was dropping with the sun. The muted pinks and oranges of dusk were starting to poke through the gray sky. "I had to sort of lead her to it. I mentioned that I'd smelled the same ointment on Amanda's skin. Then her memory was jogged, but honestly, she seemed to be natural about it all. I didn't get the sense that she was flustered or on defense. I think she just genuinely forgot. What did Susana have to say?"

"She was poring over the accounts and trying to decide if they should put on the shows after all. They'll be in the red if they have to refund tickets."

"That makes sense. Did she impart anything else of note?" I asked.

"Not really. Feeling a little lost on this case. I think I'll head back to the office and go over my notes and the coroner's report once more. Then I promised Bear a long walk."

We stopped in front of the police station. He peeked around and kissed me. "Hmm, I missed those sweet lips. Have fun at girls' night."

"Thanks. Let me know if anything pops out at you about the case." I waved and headed along the sidewalk toward the flower shop.

CHAPTER 25

*W*e'd pooled our Nicholas Sparks movies and ended up with our usual favorite, The Notebook. We'd seen it enough that we could talk through most of the movie and still know exactly what was happening. It was the perfect selection for girls' night. And so were the treats and drinks.

Lola was busy in the kitchen fixing up a tantalizing boozy drink that contained sparkling cranberry and vodka. It was rare for any of us to drink hard liquor, but Lola had seen the drink on Instagram and decided we could step out of our comfort zone for one evening. Besides, there were plenty of hearty, filling treats to absorb any of the impact of the alcohol.

Elsie had brought her promised chocolate croissants. She also had several berry tarts that had been leftover from the day's business. I fixed a hummus dip complete with pita chips and fresh veggies, and Lola, who rarely spent time in the kitchen, had stopped at the pizza restaurant for some cheesy bread and garlic sticks. It was a carb filled extravaganza.

Lola handed me the spritzy drink. My nose tickled from the bubbles. "I think I'm going to like this." I took a sip. "Hmm, I love anything bubbly. And the perfect cocktail to go with Elsie's chocolate croissant." I lifted the pastry off the plate and admired it. "Ah, who am I kidding? I'd eat this with any drink." I took a bite. The thick dark chocolate filling melted on my tongue. I followed the bite with another sip of my drink. "Culinary perfection."

Elsie filled her plate with some of the veggies and dip. She rarely ate her own baked goods at gatherings, which made sense. She was breathing the stuff in all day. Although, then what was my excuse? Most of the delicious aromas from the bakery wafted through the flower shop walls all day. Ryder only got the occasional whiff, but my super nose picked up every sugary smell.

Lola plunked down on the couch next to me with a plate piled high with goodies and her cranberry drink. Elsie sat in the chair. We'd started the movie ten minutes earlier, but the sound was on mute. Lola glanced at the screen as she picked up a pita chip. "Ryan Gosling should have left his nose alone. I mean seriously, he's so handsome with the crooked nose."

"I agree," Elsie said. "It gives him character."

"Maybe he'd been self conscious about his nose his whole life," I suggested. "Maybe he was teased, so he decided he was rich and famous enough to finally fix it. But I agree. He looks sort of cocky and charming with the crooked nose. Now, when he comes on screen, I'm not entirely sure it's him."

"Yes and then there's the whole Ryan Gosling and Ryan Reynolds confusion thing. Now he looks more like Reynolds, so it's harder to tell them apart," Elsie said.

I looked at Lola for confirmation on that theory. She shook her head, so she was with me on it. "I don't think they look that much alike, Elsie. They get confused because they have the same first name," I said.

"I think you're wrong but then what do I know?" Elsie said.

Lola dipped a carrot into hummus. "According to you—absolutely everything," she quipped.

Elsie paused in thought. "Actually, you're right. So, Lola, have you stopped torturing poor Ryder about his trip?"

Lola licked the carrot. "I might try and get a few more gifts or nice dinners out of it."

"You're wicked," I said. "If you look up the word in the dictionary, your smiling face would be sitting right next to it."

"And yet, I'm unmoved," Lola said with a chin lift. "You two should be vying for a few trinkets too. After all, you'll both have to put up with me while my boyfriend is somewhere near the equator traipsing through snake-filled jungles."

Elsie glanced my way. "Hadn't thought of that."

"Oh, I have," I admitted. "I'm already gearing up for it."

"Just like I'm gearing up for your freak out when bridal season hits and you realize you don't have my wonderful boyfriend around to keep you calm and organized." Lola sat back and bit the carrot.

Elsie rested back in the chair. "She has a point."

"Said the woman who has gone through more assistants than I've gone through toothbrushes. Oh, let's stop this, girls. I need one of those tarts." I hopped up and walked to the table where we'd laid our spread. "My appetite came back with a vengeance once that nasty cold finally disappeared."

"You got over it quick," Lola said.

"That's because I gave her a delicious healthy lunch filled with super foods." There was not even a second of hesitation when Elsie said it.

"I think Franki would argue that point. She insisted her chicken soup is the best way to cure a cold." I finally decided on a strawberry tart. It was heavy with a clear, syrupy glaze.

Lola snapped her fingers and looked my direction. "I just remembered, I was going to tell you something."

I walked around and sat next to her but swiveled to face her. "Can I listen while eating a strawberry tart?"

"Sure, knock yourself out. This afternoon, Officer Chinmoor was in my shop looking to buy an antique dresser. He was going to buy it for his girlfriend's birthday," Lola said.

Elsie snickered. "Do you mean to tell me that silly man has found himself a girlfriend?"

Lola looked askance at her. "Boy, someone is feeling catty tonight."

Elsie's head tilted with an 'oh come on' look, but Lola decided to carry on. "Anyhow, he was trying to decide between an Empire style 1840's four drawer dresser with carved feet and a midcentury walnut one that was more her style but cost an extra fifty bucks." She waved her hand. "That's beside the point. So he's standing there taking his sweet time trying to make the right decision, and these two women walk into the shop. I knew they had to be with the theater group because I'd never seen them before, and they were cute and petite and they sort of moved like dancers."

"Will this story get more interesting?" Elsie said before biting down loudly on a pita chip.

We both looked at her somewhat disapprovingly.

"Sorry," she said, "I haven't been on a run in two days, so I've got some bottled up tension. Continue with this riveting tale."

Lola shook her head. "Don't skip the run tomorrow or none of us will be talking to you next week. As I was saying, these two cute actresses walked in to browse around the shop. One of them was wearing this unbelievably cool—"

"Bomber jacket," I said.

Lola's shoulders deflated. "Yes, darn. How did you know?"

"That's Joan. She told me she got the jacket from her—"

"Grandfather," Lola said quickly. "There, we're even. As neat as the jacket was, that isn't the part I wanted to tell you. The two girls spotted Officer Chinmoor, he was in uniform, on break," she explained. "They were flipping through the old posters I have in the movie star bin, and they started talking really loudly about the murder."

"You mean like they wanted Chinmoor to hear it?" I asked.

"That was sure what it seemed like to me. I don't know why else they'd have been projecting their voices like they were onstage or something."

I scooted closer. "What did they say? What were they saying about the murder?"

"First they lamented about how they might not be paid if they have to refund the tickets. That's when the one in the bomber jacket, rather loudly, said that someone named Susana was always messing up."

Elsie had gotten pulled in to the subject matter now. "Who is Susana?" she asked.

"Susana Damon is the director," I explained. "I spotted Susana having a terrible fight with the victim, Amanda, the woman who played Dorothy. It was just hours before her murder. Susana claimed to have apologized and smoothed things over with Amanda just after the dress rehearsal."

"Well, not according to the two loud talkers," Lola interjected.

"Really?" I put my empty plate down on the coffee table. "Did they talk about the fight?"

"I don't know if this was directly related to the fight, but they said that Susana's mistakes were the reason that Amanda had been going behind Susana's back to talk the producers into firing her. According to their very public conversation, they said the producers were actually going to take Amanda up on the idea. Supposedly, there had been just too many mess ups. They said poor Susana knew her days with the troupe were numbered, and it was all because of Amanda using her clout to get what she wanted. They weren't exactly speaking fondly of the victim either."

"No, in some of my interviews, I got the feeling she was a bit of a prima donna. I must ask—how did Officer Chinmoor respond to the gossip he was overhearing? Did he walk over to ask them more questions?"

Lola pursed her mouth in thought. "No, now that you mention it—their loud conversation was all in vain. He was so involved in selecting the right dresser for his girlfriend, I'm not sure he heard a word."

"Told you he was silly," Elsie quipped.

"I guess she's right." Lola tilted her head toward Elsie. "As usual. I mean, I'm just a little old antique dealer, but I could tell they were trying very hard to implicate this woman Susana as the killer. They were certainly tossing a motive out there, dangling it for the officer, who couldn't be bothered to take the bait."

"Poor Officer Chinmoor. He tries so hard sometimes but then important stuff slips right by him." I would tell Briggs about the conversation Lola overheard, but I decided I could leave off the part about Chinmoor standing right there in the store. It was even possible he had heard the conversation but decided not to ask them questions right in the middle of the store. Officer Chinmoor liked to do stuff by the book. I pushed up from the couch and picked up the drink. "I'm going for seconds. Anyone else?"

Lola held up her glass. "Yes, please. And bring me one of those fruit tarts on your way back to the couch."

CHAPTER 26

Fortunately, I'd had the forethought to stop at two drinks on girls' night. Otherwise, I would have woken with a headache, and I had at least a dozen bouquets to create for customers. The final two, twin vases for actual twins who were turning sixty, were a sumptuous mix of red and orange roses surrounded by a collar of ivy and dotted intermittently with bright pink asters. I finished the bouquets by tying a large pale pink bow around each vase.

"I think those are your best of the morning," Ryder said as he cut the ends off a fresh shipment of roses.

I leaned back to admire them. "I think you're right. The customer should be here in the next hour to pick them up." I pulled off my work apron.

The sun was shining brightly, and it was a true spring day. A dry breeze had brought in some warm air, and it tickled the fresh new leaves on the trees. A walk to the beach was just what I needed after hours of arranging flowers.

"I could use a break. Do you mind taking over for an hour or so. I was thinking I might—"

"Snoop around at the town square?" he asked.

"You know me too well." I hung up the apron and picked up some of the debris I'd left on the work space.

"I'll get that," Ryder said. "By the way, we've been so busy all morning, you never told me how girls' night went."

I put my hands on my hips. "I'd tell you but then I'd have to kill you. You know what happens at girls' night stays at girls' night."

"Right, what was I thinking. Don't tell me then. I'm too young to die. Have a nice walk."

He seemed a little disappointed that I'd cut him off so I stopped at the door. "Not much happened except snacking, a bit of imbibing and a lot of talking. The usual. See you in an hour."

I headed down the sidewalk and was disappointed to see that Briggs' car was not parked in its usual spot. I'd hoped to stop in and say hello.

The sky over the beach reminded me of a turquoise bracelet my mom inherited from her mother. A deep breath revealed that the scent of true spring with its tickling pollen and baby fresh flowers was right around the bend. Fortunately for me, I was rarely allergic to any of the fragrances nature had to offer, with the exception of eucalyptus. I'd certainly confirmed my allergy to that fragrance in the past few days.

I turned along Pickford Way. The drooping sun was reflecting off the ivory white canvas of the performance tent. I shaded my eyes with my hand and surveyed the tent. Aside from the two front flaps where the audience walked through, there were two exit flaps at the rear, one for each side of the stage. It made sense that characters would enter from different sides of the stage. I realized I'd never sniffed around the rear exits of the tent. I assumed the evidence team did a thorough inspection, but I was sure no one had taken an actual sniff of the canvas.

As luck would have it, no one seemed to be working near the rear of the tent. I cut across the grass to the rear exit on the right.

The flaps were tied loosely together with thin canvas bows. I decided to focus on the inside edges of the flaps, the place where people would touch the canvas.

I ran my nose along it and smelled the oil they used to keep canvas supple. There was a variety of smells, everything from mustard to aftershave. Nothing significant popped out at me, and there were far too many smells to make sense of anything. Dozens of people had probably grabbed the edge of the flap. It had been silly of me to think I'd find something important.

I released the flap and something shiny caught my eye. Glitter. "Oh great, now I'm stuck with glitter." I took a closer look and noticed more than a few smudges of glitter here and there. It really was everywhere and now it was on me.

I decided to change course when I spotted Johnny Vespo without his silver makeup and funnel hat. He was walking along the wharf checking out the food stands. There was something about the guy I just didn't like or trust. I had no intention of talking to him, but I didn't want to miss an opportunity to see what the Tin Man did in his spare time. Maybe he was meeting someone on the wharf.

I hurried across Pickford Way and trotted up the steps to the wharf. I had his shiny black hair in my sights until a small moment of chaos broke out on the wharf in front of the fish market, a place my sensitive nose and I usually tried to avoid.

A group of people were circled around something. Everyone looked distraught and frantic. Between fidgeting legs and frightened steps backwards, I saw a large pair of gray wings flapping wildly.

I raced over and pushed between some of the onlookers, who were gasping and asking each other what to do. A large pelican had managed to get himself tangled up in fishing line. His massive beak was clapping at the air, as it took short, anxious breaths. The poor thing was about to scare itself into a heart attack.

I didn't hesitate. The bird stumbled sideways and clapped its beak at me. Its beady eyes watched me with fear and mistrust. One of the men watching helplessly from the sidelines had a bucket of freshly caught fish.

"Please, if you don't mind. I can use a fish to keep his beak occupied," I said.

Everyone prodded the reluctant fisherman to give up a fish. It was slippery and cold in my hand as I held the fish out for the terrified bird. "It's all right," I said in dulcet tones, the same ones I used when Kingston was frightened of something. The pelican responded. His breathing slowed and he turned his beak toward the fish. I dropped it into the pouch and set instantly to work untangling the lines. They were just beginning to cut into his belly. With some effort, I managed to get him free of his predicament. I stood with the clump of plastic line in my hand and everyone clapped. The noise sent the pelican into the air. He soared across to one of the pylons on the pier to finish his fish.

I broke free of the small crowd and searched up and down the wharf. I'd lost sight of Johnny. I headed toward the marina hoping I'd spot him somewhere along the boat slips. I gasped when someone grabbed my hand. I spun around and came face to face with the man I'd been following.

"There's nothing I love more than a brave woman," Johnny said with a smarmy smile. "That was something how you walked right up to that bird and saved its life. You could have been hurt." He still hadn't released my hand, so I took the liberty of yanking it free.

"I was in no danger. The bird was just scared, that's all. He wouldn't have hurt me."

Yanking my hand away was not a big enough hint, apparently.

He stepped closer. He was wearing pungent cologne, and the grease slicking back his dark hair had a fragrance of its own. The two mixed together were making my eyes water.

"I can't believe we nearly smacked into each other again. It must be fate." He reached up and tried to touch my hair.

I leaned back. "Please don't touch me or my hair. And it wasn't fate because we didn't smack into each other. You grabbed my hand. Rudely, I might add. Now, I've got somewhere to be." I turned but he grabbed my hand again.

"Let go of the lady's hand," a familiar, deep voice said from behind. I looked over my shoulder. My neighbor and friend, Dash, was standing with his arms crossed and his feet set hard on the wood planks.

"Why don't you mind your own business," Johnny said.

I yanked my hand free again. "And why don't you take a big old in your face rejection as the final word?" I stepped back to where Dash was standing.

Dash kept his piercing gaze on Johnny to make sure the thick-headed man got the point. He finally marched away without another word.

"Thank you, Dash. The nerve of that guy."

The angry veneer on his face cracked enough to give me a look of concern. He looked at my hand. "He didn't hurt you, did he?"

I lifted my hand to assure him all the fingers were still moving. "No, I'm fine. Just a little shaken. He came up so suddenly. Good thing you happened by."

"I don't know, I think you probably could have handled it. I especially liked that last zinger you threw at him."

"Guess it was pretty good since I came up with it in the midst of a tense moment. Where were you heading?" I asked.

"Actually, I was working on an engine, and the boat's owner told me some fearless woman just untangled a pelican from fishing line. He mentioned he thought it was the town florist, so I figured I'd walk down and say hello to the fearless woman." His Hollywood caliber smile appeared. "Hello."

"Hello, and I wouldn't say I'm fearless. After all, you know how I feel about the dark."

"Yes but that's entirely reasonable. A lot of people are afraid of the dark. What brings you down to the wharf this afternoon? Hoping for a chat with your impossibly charming neighbor?"

I laughed. It felt good to know the entire unpleasant scene was behind me. "I'm always up for a chat with my impossibly charming neighbor, but if I'm being honest, I was actually following that creep who just grabbed my hand. I'd lost sight of him when I stopped to help the pelican. Then, apparently, he was following me."

"Stay away from that guy. He's bad news. This wasn't the first time I saw him get grabby with a woman." Dash motioned with his head. "I'll walk you back to Pickford Way. I'm on a break."

I looked out at the pier. The pelican was long gone, hopefully soaring over the waves and staying clear of fishing line and nets. "What do you mean? You've seen him do this before?"

"I was working on a boat in the marina on Thursday morning. That guy was walking along the wharf with the actress who was killed. He had her up against the railing. At first, she was giggling and seemed to be enjoying the attention so I went back to my work. Then I heard things get heated. She told him to leave her alone, and she shoved him back. Then she ducked under his arm and hurried away. He looked pretty mad, but he didn't go after her. He paced the wharf for a few minutes. That was the last I saw of him."

"A guy like that obviously doesn't take rejection well," I said more to myself. "Although, she might have made up with him later. One of my customers saw the Tin Man and Dorothy in full costume cozy on a wharf bench. But maybe she misread the inter-action." Either way Amanda sure seemed to be involved in a tangled soap opera when it came to her male coworkers. "Did you tell the police what you saw? It might be relevant."

"I walked to the station on Friday. Briggs was out so I relayed what I saw to Officer Chinmoor. Not sure if it went anywhere after that."

"I'll have to ask Briggs if Chinmoor filled him in. Officer Chinmoor means well and tries hard but—"

"But he's sort of the Barney of Mayberry."

I stifled a laugh, but it was probably a good analogy.

We passed the place where I'd helped the pelican. A few of the people standing around pointed and said something like 'there she is, that's the lady who saved the pelican'.

Dash chuckled. "Looks like you're famous."

"Maybe they'll put a plaque on the pier with my picture and underneath it'll read 'the lady who saved the pelican'."

Dash stopped at the steps leading down to the street. "I'm going to head back to the marina."

"Thank you again, Dash. And thanks for the information. Maybe my walk along the wharf wasn't a complete loss after all."

CHAPTER 27

I hadn't made it ten steps on Pickford Way when Constance came scurrying out of seemingly nowhere to talk to me. She kept peeking around in a paranoid fashion as if she worried someone might see her talking to me. She seemed distraught and not herself.

"Lacey, I was looking for you. I saw you earlier but then you vanished."

"I was taking a walk on the wharf. What can I do for you? You seem upset."

She pressed her hand to her chest. "Yes, it's just I've discovered something that I think I should show someone. But since I can't trust anyone in the group"—she leaned closer—"you know, in case one of them is the killer, I spotted you and since you're with Detective Briggs—" Her breath was coming in short spurts as she tried to get it all out.

I put my hand on her arm. "Slow down and take a breath. Then you can show me, and I'll talk to Detective Briggs. No one from the theater group needs to know."

Constance nodded and paused dramatically to catch her breath. "Thank you. I feel so much better. I'm glad I saw you again. I was so frantic after I lost sight of you earlier." Her little chin tilted to the side. "Were you inspecting the tent? I thought I saw you at the back, near the stage entrances." Her big eyes grew larger. "Did you find anything? Maybe you saw the same thing I saw."

I wasn't exactly sure how to lie my way out of snooping around the tent, so I went with the truth. "I was just checking to see if the evidence team missed anything."

"That's right. You told me you have an extra good sense of smell. Did you find anything? It sure would be nice if they arrested the killer so the rest of us can sleep better."

"I'm sure it'll happen soon. And no, I didn't find anything. But it sure seems like you did. What did you discover?"

She shrank down and peeked around. There was plenty of activity in the town square, but no one seemed the least bit interested in what Constance was doing. They were all going about their business. I did a quick visual sweep of the area, keeping a particular eye out for Johnny. I was relieved not to see him.

"What I have to show you is inside the performance tent," Constance said in a low voice. "Let's walk to the end of the side-walk and cut across to the back of the tent so no one sees us."

"All right." I had no idea what she would show me considering the entire stage and tent had been searched for evidence the night of the murder. Whatever it was, Constance seemed to think it was important.

Like spies sneaking into the enemy's headquarters, we hunkered down to be less visible. With furtive glances both directions, we skittered across the grass and then raced to the back of the tent. Even though we should have drawn attention with our obvious run, it seemed we made it to the stage entrance without notice.

We stopped at the flaps. Constance put a finger to her lips, telling me to be silent. Then she untied a few of the bows and poked her face into the tent. She pulled it back out. "Coast is clear. There's no one inside." She quickly opened the remaining ties and we slipped into the tent. She pushed the flaps closed to give the appearance that they were still tied shut.

We climbed the three steps to the stage. The first scene, Aunt Em's farmstead, was set up. "Remember when you saw me painting the farmhouse?" she asked, still using a library voice.

I nodded. "Yes, I remember."

We sidled past a barn and a few trees to the farmhouse. It was the same large wooden facade that had fallen on Amanda after her death. It was never completely confirmed how the prop fell or if it was done intentionally by the killer.

"We finished repairing it after it was damaged." Constance grew quiet for a second. "Well, you know why."

"Yes."

"I was helping the prop guys wheel it in to set it back in place on the stage." She crooked her finger for me to follow her to the back of the farmhouse. The rear was unpainted plywood, which made it hard to miss the shiny piece of foil stuck on the wood.

We walked straight to the silver paper. It was the thin metallic kind that artists used to give an object the look of real metal. The roughly edged strip was approximately four inches long and two inches wide. It was caught on the wood edge of the facade. It had plastered itself against the bare wood.

"I noticed the piece of silver when we were positioning the house on stage," Constance said. "I know where it came from too," she added.

"My guess would be that it came from the Tin Man's costume," I said.

"Yep, I can show you the damage on his costume," she said confidently. "It's stored in the costume trailer."

"If you're sure you won't get into trouble. I would like to see it."

She glanced at her phone. "Yes, it'll be easy. The costume designer and wardrobe assistants are in a staff meeting with Susie. But we'll have to hurry."

"Great." I pulled out my own phone. "If you don't mind, before we go, I'd like to take a few pictures of this silver. That way, I can show Detective Briggs."

"Yes," she said a little too enthusiastically. "Yes," she said calmly. "That would be fine."

I wasn't great at taking pictures of evidence, so I took a half dozen shots at different angles.

I pushed the phone back into my pocket. "Let's see the costume."

We walked back to the exit and did everything in reverse. Constance stuck her face through and turned it side to side to make sure the coast was clear. She stepped out and waved me through before tying the flaps back together.

We walked more casually, as if just on a stroll, around the tent. We continued on the pathway toward the costume trailer. A few people seemed to notice the unusual pair walking through the activity, but Constance just smiled and waved as if nothing of note was going on.

Fortunately, the costume trailer had been parked behind a copse of trees. It was hard to see the door from the pathway. We stepped off the path and meandered toward the trees.

Constance glanced back behind us. "It's fine. No one is paying attention to us." She picked up her pace, making quick work of the section of grass between us and the trailer. "Let me go up first and knock," she said. "I can always find a reason for knocking on the trailer door, but it would be harder to explain why you're here."

I nodded. "You're pretty good at this spy stuff," I said. "Maybe you should become a private investigator."

She giggled at my suggestion before climbing the steps to the door. She knocked firmly and waited, then knocked once more. She waved me to come up the steps.

I looked around once and followed her up the steps and into the trailer. It was a tiny space packed wall to wall and shelf to shelf with colorful costumes and hats. There was an entire section of wall filled with pairs of flying monkey wings hanging from hooks. They'd been fashioned with real feathers and were quite impressive close up.

"Your costume designers are talented," I said as I looked around in awe.

"Yes, they are. The producers spared no expense for this traveling play. We were doing well until this happened." She said it flippantly as if Amanda's death had been a terrible inconvenience to everyone.

"Will the show go on?" I asked.

"I'm pretty sure Susana will have no choice but to reschedule opening night and the subsequent shows." Constance looked more than delighted at the prospect. I supposed that was because she would step into the starring role.

Constance squeezed between two racks of costumes, and I slid in after her. The fuzzy tan costume for the Cowardly Lion was hanging in the middle of the rack. The long tail was pinned to the shoulder. It was easy to spot the Tin Man's iconic cylindrical costume. Especially after I'd run right into it on the corner. When I thought back to that incident, Johnny acted inappropriately and forward then too. He was obviously a man who considered himself entitled to paw at any woman he pleased.

Constance sized up the tight space between the two racks. "You'll have to squeeze past me to get a look at the tear. It's on the back near the shoulder joint."

"Right. Can I take a picture?"

"Sure, but just like before, let's be quick about this. The meeting could end at any time. It depends on how much Susie has to discuss."

"I'll hurry." Giddiness was starting to overtake me, the kind I experienced whenever I felt close to solving a crime. It seemed that the evidence Constance was showing me would be explosive to the case. It would figure that grabby, awful man would be capable of murder.

I squeezed past Constance and reached the Tin Man's suit. "Rosemary," I said under my breath. "That should have been the clue."

"What's that?" Constance asked. She had slid out to the end of the rack to keep an eye on the window.

"Oh nothing." I leaned over and twisted around the silver cylinder. Sure enough, a section that matched the piece of silver paper on the house had been ripped from the costume. I held up my phone and snapped a couple highly unprofessional photos.

"We should probably go," Constance said with some urgency.

"Finished. Let's go."

Constance peered out the door and looked from side to side. She opened it and we both hurried down the steps and back to the copse of trees. Constance seemed as giddy as me.

"Do you think this is going to be important to the case? Do you think Johnny did it?" she asked.

"This doesn't prove anything," I said quickly. "Make sure you don't say anything to anyone. It could compromise the case."

"So Johnny did do it?" She was practically rubbing her hands together in glee, which made me wonder if Constance had also been the victim of Johnny's unwanted advances.

"No, I didn't say that at all."

Her mouth pushed out in a disappointed pout. "How can you explain the silver on the house?"

"I'll admit this doesn't look great for Johnny, but it's not enough for an arrest. I'll show Detective Briggs the photos. In the meantime, keep it to yourself. If Johnny is the killer, I don't want you putting yourself in danger by telling others what you've found."

She pressed her fingers to her mouth dramatically. "I hadn't thought of that. Thanks. You're right. Mums the word." She surveyed the area. "You go first. Then I'll walk out after you so we're not seen leaving together."

"Good idea. Thanks for the information."

CHAPTER 28

I practically skipped back to Harbor Lane and the Port Danby Police Department. I gave a little cheer when I saw Briggs' car parked out front. I pulled open the door.

Hilda peered up over the tall counter to see who had walked inside. "Lacey, I haven't seen you in ages." She stood up. "Have you lost weight?"

"You always know just the right thing to say to make my day, Hilda, and I wish I could give you an affirmative on that but I think I'm about the same."

"Well, you have a perfect shape anyhow." Hilda hit the buzzer to open the gate. "He's in his office."

"Thanks." I knocked lightly and popped my head inside.

"Hey, I was just about to call you," Briggs said. His big, loveable dog came prancing around the desk to greet me.

"Bear, what an unexpected pleasure." I stooped down to hug the dog and receive a proper amount of wet kisses. "Why is he here?"

"Well, his usual babysitter, my neighbor, had a doctor's appointment. I was about to walk out the door and leave him alone with his chew toy and pillow, but he stared up at me with those big, sad eyes. So I decided to bring him to work. It's like one of those bring your kids to work days only my kid has big floppy ears and clumsy paws."

After a reasonable amount of hugs and kisses, I stood up straight. "How is the case going?" I asked, unable to hold back the excitement in my tone.

Briggs noticed. He suppressed a smile as he walked around to the front of his desk and leaned against it with crossed arms and ankles. "Not too sure but I think you're about to tell me. You look like you're bursting to tell me something."

"I might have some evidence that'll lead to an eventual arrest." I decided to draw out the suspense a bit.

"I sure hope so because the person at the top of my list, Gordon Houser, has been cleared by some of his coworkers. I questioned several today. They all said he was on stage at 3:30, so he couldn't have sent the text to Amanda."

"This evidence has to do with another cast member, Johnny Vespo, the Tin Man."

"Really? What did you find out? I hope you're not doing anything dangerous," he added unnecessarily at the end.

I tilted my head. "Really?"

He sighed. "You're right. Sorry. What did you find out?"

I pulled out my phone. "It'll be easier to show you first." I pulled up the best photo of the silver paper. "Constance, the actress you met, who I told you was dating Gordon Houser, ran into me when I was down by the town square. She was quite distressed when she caught up to me because she had discovered that piece of silver on the back of the house, Aunt Em's farmhouse that fell on Amanda." I grinned with satisfaction.

Briggs stared at the picture for a moment then looked at me. "I don't understand the significance."

My satisfied grin melted. "Seriously? The Tin Man, somehow or another, ripped his costume on the very prop that the killer pushed onto his victim. There haven't been any shows or rehearsals since that night, so when would he have ripped the costume? And I saw the costume too." I was speaking quickly not wanting to lose my somewhat disinterested audience. I swiped through the photos to the costume and pushed it toward his face. He leaned back and squinted at the picture.

"Yes, that looks like the Tin Man's costume, and I'd say there's no question that the silver paper on the prop came from that costume."

I lowered my phone. My earlier giddiness was flowing away. Had I jumped to conclusions because I was disgusted with Johnny Vespo and his rude behavior? "I was sure this was significant."

"Lacey, I inspected that whole set along with the team. I don't see how we could have missed that piece of silver paper. It must have happened afterward."

"We just need to ask Susana or someone if there's been any dress rehearsals or reasons to suit up since Thursday night. She can confirm whether or not Johnny had to wear his costume since that night. But since Constance was the one to point it out, it seems like she would have brought up getting in costume since opening night." I could hear myself on the defensive, but I felt strongly about the evidence. I couldn't figure out why he didn't seem convinced.

"Just doesn't make sense that we missed that very noticeable piece of silver, but let's go there right now so I can see its exact location. Maybe it was overlooked. Stranger things have happened. Can you take the time to go with me, or have you already spent your entire break snooping around town square?"

"Let me text Ryder and make sure he doesn't need me. I don't want to miss seeing your face when you see that piece of silver sitting plain as day on the back of that house."

He patted Bear on the head. "I'll certainly be second guessing my detective abilities if I missed that major piece of evidence."

"Maybe I'll have to teach you what I know," I quipped as we headed out of the office.

CHAPTER 29

I spoke with the Tin Man actor a few times," Briggs said on our walk to the town square. "He comes off as cocky and a know it all, but he had a few witnesses to corroborate that he went back to his trailer right after dress rehearsal."

"But did anyone see him after that?" I was still actively trying to find a good reason for Briggs to arrest Johnny Vespo. At the same time, I was trying to convince myself it wasn't because of the incident on the wharf. I hadn't mentioned it to Briggs and was still debating whether I should bring it up. Would it help or hurt my case? It would definitely make Briggs mad, but I needed him to think with a cool head. I didn't want to be the cause of a false arrest.

"I don't have confirmation or denial on that," he said. "Let's see what we find out."

We rounded the corner to Pickford Way. A boy about ten years old pointed at me and tugged at his mom's sleeve. "Look, Mom, it's the lady who saved the pelican."

It seemed my fifteen minutes of fame hadn't faded yet. Briggs was staring at the side of my face as I tried to nonchalantly continue our walk.

"You saved a pelican? My word, woman, when do you find time in the day?"

"I guess I don't waste a minute of my life."

"Would you like to tell me about it?" he asked.

It was my opportunity to bring up the incident on the wharf. I hoped it would shed some light on Johnny's character.

We stopped just before reaching the town square. "The pelican story wasn't all that impressive. The poor bird was caught in some fishing line and I untangled it. Now, you may ask *why* I was on the wharf helping out a bird and I will tell you, but you must promise not to blow your stack."

He laughed dryly. "Blow my stack?"

"You heard me."

"Fine, I'll keep my stack on. What happened?"

"I was snooping around the theater tent but found nothing." Before he could mention the silver I spoke up. "I didn't go inside, so I wouldn't have seen the silver. But I spotted Johnny Vespo walking along the wharf. I decided to follow him, discretely, just to see what he was up to. I wondered if maybe he was meeting someone. I'm not really sure why but there was rosemary on the victim and on the Tin Man, and the guy just has this unlikeable way about him. So I followed him, keeping my distance like a good investigator. Then the whole pelican thing happened, and I stopped to be the 'lady who saved the pelican'. There's going to be a plaque and everything." I waved my hand. "Anyhow, that detour caused me to lose sight of my target. I couldn't find Johnny, but I decided to head toward the marina in case he had wandered through the boat slips. Then someone grabbed my hand."

I caught a flicker in his dark eyes. He was working hard to keep that stack on, whatever that meant. "Go on," he said, his jaw tighter than normal.

"Remember your promise," I said fleetingly, then poured out the rest of it. "Johnny had grabbed my hand. He saw me help the pelican, apparently, so *he* followed me."

"What did he want?" His words were dry and short.

"I don't know. I guess he was being forward. I yanked my hand away, but he grabbed it again."

His jaw was clenched tighter now.

I pointed at it. "See, see that thing you're doing with your jaw, that indicates a stack being blown. But don't waste your energy. It was fine. I finally told him to bug off and he did." I almost left out the part where Dash stared him down with a threatening glare. Since Dash was one of Briggs least favorite people, I knew it would only cause problems. But Dash had witnessed a similar incident between Johnny and Amanda. And while he'd relayed what he saw to Officer Chinmoor, I got the feeling Chinmoor never told his boss.

I peered up at Briggs. Trying to assess his level of tension. He was wound pretty tight, but I needed to tell him the rest.

"There's more," I said meekly. "But it's not about me."

He seemed to release a breath he'd been holding. "Go on."

"During my little incident with Johnny—"

"Adding in the word *little* doesn't make me less mad."

"It was worth a shot. Anyhow, I had a little—" I cleared my throat. "I had help getting rid of Johnny. Dash happened to see the whole thing. He basically glared Johnny right off the wharf."

His jaw twitch remained steady. "Of all the names you could have added to make this story less aggravating, it was *that* one."

I put my hands on my hips. "He was there to help, or did you miss that part?"

He gave a half-hearted nod. "I'm glad he stepped in."

"Me too. He also had a tidbit of information about Johnny. Dash said he saw Johnny with Amanda on the wharf on Thursday morning. They seemed to just be flirting at first, then things got tense. Amanda had to push him away to get free of him. Dash said after the murder he stopped in to tell Officer Chinmoor what he witnessed. Did Chinmoor ever tell you about it?"

He rubbed his chin in thought. "No, I would have remembered that." His sigh was heavy with frustration. "I'll have to talk to Chinmoor about that."

"So, you see, Johnny's not a nice guy, and it seems Amanda rejected him that morning. Something I learned, firsthand, he doesn't take kindly to." It was a mistake to bring up my involvement again, but I couldn't draw the words back in once they were out.

"I'd like to talk to this guy, Johnny." Briggs started walking purposefully toward the theater action.

I grabbed his arm to stop him. "How does a man who stays poker face calm when questioning possible murderers lose his cool so quickly with a simple story that turned out to be harmless?"

His dark eyes flickered with emotion for a second. Then he nodded in agreement. "Right, let's find the evidence to arrest him. Then he's all mine."

I blew out a loud sigh. "Glad we smoothed that out," I said wryly.

"It's your fault," he said as we continued on toward the tent.

"What's my fault?"

"My reaction. Guess the only way to avoid it is for me to stop caring about you so much."

I stumbled at his words. He caught my arm and pulled me closer for a second. "Do you want me to stop caring about you so much?"

My throat tightened. All I could do was shake my head once.

"Good. Now let's get our killer."

This time no sneaking around the back of the tent was required. Two men were working on straightening the audience chairs inside the tent. Briggs just flashed his badge, and they went about their task as we headed up to the stage.

"Seems like they're getting ready to put on the play after all," I said.

"Looks that way," Briggs said. "Maybe we can talk to Susana after this to find out exactly what's going on."

"It's right over here," I walked between the fake trees and shrubs to the back of Aunt Em's farmhouse. The piece of silver shimmered in the overhead lights strung across the tent. Briggs stopped and stared at the piece for a long moment.

"Well?" I asked.

"It's certainly there, shiny and very noticeable, but I walked around these props on this opening scene set five or six times. I don't see how I could have possibly missed this shiny object. And it's not small. The evidence team scoured this stage. How could they have missed it too? We need to ask Susana if the actors have been in costume since that night."

"If not, which I suspect is the case only because I've walked through town square several times since then and I never saw anyone in costume, then how do we explain this?"

He shook his head. "Maybe someone put it there. Sounds like Johnny Vespo is pretty despicable. Maybe someone wanted to frame him. Let's go over to the trailer where they store the Tin Man costume so I can get a look at it."

Again, there was no need to sneak under trees or dash to doors. That shiny detective's badge was like a magic key to everything. Briggs pulled it out, prepared to show whoever was working in the costume trailer.

"You sure have it easier than me when it comes to this investigating stuff. I have to dodge people and hide in shadows just to snoop around, whereas you just flash the pretty piece of metal and people step aside and invite you in."

"That's not always the case, unfortunately, but after your story about the wharf it doesn't make me feel any better to hear you say you're dodging people and hiding in shadows."

I waved it off. "I'm exaggerating, of course. I don't dodge people, I merely make a wide berth around them and as for the shadows—" My voice trailed off as Briggs knocked on the trailer door.

"Come in," a voice called.

Briggs opened the door. A woman with teased blonde hair and pinkish highlights was standing at a fold out work table with a brush full of a pungent substance (at least pungent to me) glue or shellac or possibly decoupage glaze. The unwieldy silver cylinder, the body for the Tin Man costume, was resting on the table. She'd used a few books to keep it from rolling side to side.

The woman was a little surprised at her visitors. "Hello," she said tentatively. "I'm Olivia. How can I help you?" she asked.

Briggs showed his badge as he approached the table. "Actually, I came here to look at the costume on the table. That is part of the Tin Man right?"

She laughed briefly. "Well, it ain't Toto." Another laugh followed. I had to join her. (It was funny.)

Briggs was in a darker mood after my confession about the Johnny incident, so he was all business. "Are you repairing it?"

She held up the brush filled with glue and picked up a large strip of thin silver paper. "Yes, I noticed a rip in the silver when I was inspecting the costumes. It must have happened when it was being hung on the rack."

Briggs walked to the table, and she pointed out the rip. "Why do you think it happened then?" he asked.

She shrugged. "I could be wrong. It's possible Johnny ripped it during dress rehearsal. It's just I usually notice those things when I'm collecting up costumes. It was a pretty big rip with an entire piece missing. I might have been too upset that night to notice it."

She seemed to seriously be questioning how she missed seeing the damage.

"Have the actors worn their costumes since opening night?" I asked.

"Absolutely not. As you can imagine, it's quite an ordeal getting everyone in costume. These have all been hanging right here since Thursday night when my team and I collected them."

"Thank you. That answers all my questions," Briggs said.

"You're the detective working on Amanda's murder," she said as we headed out. "Hope you catch them soon."

"If I had a dollar for every time I heard that," Briggs muttered to me as we walked out of the trailer. "People think I can just snap my fingers, and the perpetrator will step out of nowhere with a signed confession."

I sensed he was still feeling grouchy about my wharf incident. I was regretting sharing it with him, only I thought it important to lay out Johnny's somewhat despicable character. The new evidence didn't seem nearly as damning as it was when I walked into the police station. None of it really made sense. The team and Briggs himself had examined the stage and the props. How would they have missed the strip of silver? On top of that, it seemed unlikely that Olivia and her crew would have missed the noticeable rip when they were carefully hanging and storing the costumes.

"What are you thinking?" I asked.

"At the moment, nothing too intriguing," he said dejectedly. "Not sure which direction to go with this. Let's go talk to Susana. I've got a few questions for her."

CHAPTER 30

*B*riggs and I trekked across the grass to the director's trailer and were surprised to see Mayor Price leaving. He was wearing an enormous grin, a rarity for him. (At least whenever I was in the vicinity.) He spotted us but, amazingly, his grin didn't fade. He also strode past us without a word or a glance our direction.

"I'm feeling rather invisible," Briggs said. "But then that's not always a bad thing."

"I agree."

We hadn't reached the steps before the trailer door opened again and Susana came out. She looked equally pleased about something and just distracted enough that she too nearly passed us by.

"Oh, Detective Briggs," she said as she looked up from her thoughts. "I suppose Mayor Price told you the news."

Briggs cleared his throat lightly. "No, we must have just missed him. What news?"

"We're going to open the show. Opening night will be tomorrow. I'm just about to call an emergency meeting to let everyone know we're back in production."

"Do you think that's wise?" Briggs asked. "Someone in your theater group very likely murdered your lead actress."

Susana lifted her chin. "I have a business to run, Detective Briggs. If we refund the tickets, the theater group will not recover financially. And how is that investigation going?" she asked a little snippily. "Are you any closer to finding the killer?"

"We're working on it. Sometimes a case like this requires a little more cooperation from the people involved," Briggs said.

Her mouth pulled tight. "Haven't we all been cooperating? I've allowed you unfettered access to cast and crew."

"Yes, you have. By cooperation, I mean people need to be a little more forthright about relationships and character flaws. What can you tell me about Johnny Vespo?"

"Johnny?" she seemed genuinely surprised. "Well, he's a good actor. He plays the Tin Man, and he's generally an audience favorite."

"I'm not interested so much in his career and talents as in his character in general. I have reason to believe that Mr. Vespo can be too forward with women. Have you witnessed anything like that?"

She paused and pursed her lips as if trying not to speak.

"This is exactly what I mean by cooperation," Briggs said tersely. He was in a much saltier mood than usual, but that was my fault. I had to admit, I didn't mind occasionally seeing this tough, gritty side of him.

"Johnny has had a few complaints filed against him," she admitted begrudgingly. "But in the end it was taken care of. Johnny promised to get some counseling, and he issued apologies to the women."

I was still feeling chafed enough by the hand grabbing incident that I decided to step in. Something told me, Briggs wouldn't mind. "You said he promised to get counseling. Did he ever give you any confirmation of that, or did you just assume he did it?"

Susana grew visibly flustered, and a red blush rose up her neck to her face. "I didn't get any official confirmation, if that's what you mean."

"Is there such thing as unofficial confirmation?" Briggs asked.

It was obvious from the pained expression, a far cry from the smile she wore when she left the trailer, that she sorely wished she hadn't run into us. "Johnny told me he attended classes, and I know him well enough to accept his word."

Briggs pulled out a notebook. "Do you have the names of the women who filed the complaints?"

"They're no longer with the troupe. They left us over a year ago."

"Because of Johnny?" I asked too eagerly.

Her brows bunched up. "No, they both landed parts in New York. Their departures had nothing to do with Johnny."

"Susie, Susie." I recognized Constance's cheery tone. She sounded a little like a happy bird. "Is it true?" she blurted before she realized that Susie was engaged in a conversation. Constance smiled at me. "Hello." She nodded at Briggs, then turned to Susana. "Rumor has it we're opening tomorrow night."

"Yes but please don't go spreading it around yet, Constance. I'm calling a meeting to make the formal announcement." Susana turned back to us. "Now, if you have no further questions, I need to talk to my cast and crew."

"Actually"—Briggs glanced at Constance, who quickly got the message and hurried away—"Did Amanda ever put in a complaint about Johnny? What exactly was their relationship?"

"Amanda never put in a complaint about Johnny. As far as I know they were friends. Possibly even more than friends."

"More than friends?" he asked.

"Detective Briggs, we're on the road most of the year. It's

impossible to form relationships with people outside this group, so there are lots of pairings and breakups and all the drama you might expect in a group traveling together across the country."

Briggs put away his notebook. "Yes, that makes sense. We won't take up any more of your time."

"Thank you." With that, she hurried away.

I needed to get to the shop so we headed back. "Penny for your thoughts, Detective Briggs," I said as we rounded the corner to Harbor Lane.

"At this point, they aren't even worth a penny. But I think I'm going to talk to Johnny Vespo. I'll ask him how his costume got ruined and mention that he was seen harassing the victim on the wharf. We'll see how he responds."

CHAPTER 31

I plodded into the flower shop feeling very deflated as compared to an hour earlier when I was taking photos of what I was sure would be incriminating evidence. But something wasn't right about any of it. Briggs and his team would never have missed that piece of silver, which meant it landed there after the murder scene was cleared. But since no one, and in particular the Tin Man, had put on costumes since that night, it meant someone must have put the silver there. It had to be someone who was trying to frame Johnny. But who?

"I thought you'd come back from your walk refreshed, but you look down in the dumps," Ryder noted. He was at the potting table. Gigi and Tom had requested some mint plants for their new herb display. I could smell the minty freshness all the way across the store.

"I walked to the town square hoping to find something to help the case. I thought I'd found it, the smoking gun, as they say, but I'm thinking it was more of a fizzled wet gun."

"Didn't pan out, eh?"

"Not really. Sort of back to square one." I grabbed the treat can and gave one to Kingston. "Your mom saved one of your kind today," I told the crow. "Well, not *your* kind specifically, but you would have been proud."

Kingston ignored me and nibbled his treat.

"You saved another crow?" Ryder asked.

"No, a pelican from some fishing line. Then it turned into a whole thing but it's over. I thought we had the killer, but now I'm not too sure."

"You'll get him. There's no better sleuth than my boss," Ryder said brightly.

"My mood might not be great, but it seems like you're doing better. Did Lola finally come to terms with the whole idea of you going off on the internship?"

"If by coming to terms you mean she hasn't been crying every time I bring it up then I guess so." Ryder turned off the sink at the potter's table. "I think I'm allergic to the mint plants. I've got a rash on my hands."

Ryder's statement pulled me out of my deep thoughts. "You do? Let me see." I walked over to the potting table. He held up his hands. Small red bumps had popped up on his wrists.

"We should get you some cream or antihistamine. Is this your first time around mint plants?"

"I think I've been around them before, but I've never trans-planted twenty plants. That takes a great deal more interaction. Maybe that's why I sneeze after I eat a peppermint. I guess I have some kind of mint allergy."

"Yes, that's just like my allergy to eucalyptus. I sneeze every time I get near it." The flat of tiny mint plants was empty. "Looks like you finished. I'll do the next mint plants if they order more. I can go to the drug store and get you some cream for that rash." I stopped and glanced back at his hands. "The rash," I said to myself.

Ryder started cleaning up the potting table. "Don't worry about the rash or the cream. My mom keeps a well-stocked medicine cabinet. She'll have something in her mini drug store to take care of the rash."

"That's good. Why don't you take off then. I'll clean the shop and lock up." My brain had had a sudden light bulb moment, and I was now anxious to close the store and head down to the station.

"I'll just clean up the mess I made," Ryder said.

"No really, go home and take care of that rash, and thank you. I think you might just have helped me solve the murder case."

Ryder's eyes lit up. "Really? Well, aren't I clever. What did I do to help you solve it?"

"It's your allergy to mint and that terrible, wonderful rash. I'll tell you all about it if it pans out, but for now, go home and take care of it."

He shook his head in confusion but followed my orders. He grabbed his coat off the hook. "See you tomorrow then, boss. And I hope you catch the killer."

"I hope so too." As soon as Ryder left, I pulled out my phone and dialed Briggs.

"Hey, I was just about to call you," he said. "I just interviewed Johnny Vespo. Looks like I won't get the pleasure of arresting him. He insisted the costume was in perfect shape when he brought it back to the costume trailer. He had a witness to corroborate it too. The costume is not easy to put on alone, so he has one of the stage hands help him get dressed and undressed. I talked to the guy who helped him undress. He said the costume was intact."

I picked up a wet rag to finish cleaning the potting counter. "Yes, that doesn't surprise me. Someone was trying to frame him. And I think I know who. I just need to solidify some details and motive."

"Are you going to fill me in on this new theory?" he asked.

"Too much to explain over the phone. I'm just cleaning up, then I'll head down to the station. I can tell you my theory then." I dried the sink and headed over to the broom.

"I won't be here. I've got to head over to the Mayfield precinct. They need me to sign off on some cases."

I stopped my awkward one handed sweeping. "Darn. I'm still going to head over to the station. I need to look at the coroner's report for Amanda. Can you leave it on your desk?"

"It's already there in the case folder. What are you looking for?"

"Would Nate make a comment or notation if he saw any rashes on Amanda's skin?"

"Sure. He's very thorough."

"Great."

"You're looking for a rash?" he asked.

"Yes and like I said, I'll explain it all when I see you. I think that first sneeze when I examined Amanda's body might just have been the only clue we needed. I want to finish cleaning, and it's impossible to sweep with one hand. I'll see you soon."

"All right and Lacey—" he started but I finished for him.

"I know. Stay out of danger."

"Right."

"You're a bit of a spoil sport, do you know that, Detective Briggs?"

"Lacey."

"Yes, yes, no danger. I'll talk to you soon."

CHAPTER 32

My feet could barely keep up with my stride as I raced along the sidewalk to the police station. My intuition usually kicked in when I was certain I stumbled on something crucial, and it was that same intuition that had sent my sleuthing sense into overdrive. This time, I was certain I had something big.

As much as I loved talking to Franki, I was slightly disappointed when she waved to me as she was getting into her car in the diner parking lot. I was bursting with frenetic energy, anxious to read the coroner's report. It could make or break my theory. Franki hurried over to me.

"It's the first shift with Kimi and Kylie in charge." Franki's terrible ex-husband had left her to fend for herself with not one but two sets of twins. They were all teens and wonderful kids. She had done a great job all around and shown her ex-husband that it was his loss. The boys, Taylor and Tyler, were away at college. Fortunately for Franki, Taylor had been quite the academic and Tyler an exceptional soccer player. They both received hefty scholarships which helped offset the cost of sending two kids to college at once. Kimi and Kylie still had a few years before college. In the meantime, Franki was training them on how to manage the diner so that Franki could take some much earned time off.

"So you left them on their own, eh? I'm sure you'll be pleased with how they handle it. They're both so smart and responsible."

Franki leaned her head side to side to let me know she wasn't entirely sure that was true. "They're good girls, and I know they want to impress me."

"What will you do with your free time?" I asked.

She rolled in her lips to hide a smile. "I've got an appointment to have a pedicure and a massage over in Mayfield."

"Good for you, Franki. You've earned it." I took a step leading away to let her know I needed to get going.

"Where are you off to in such a hurry?" she asked. "You were practically racing down the sidewalk."

"I need to look at something for the murder case." I'd found it was always best to leave out words like coroner's report and body when talking to people outside the investigative business.

"James hasn't found the killer yet? Two of the girls from the theater group just walked into the diner as I was walking out. It seemed they were excited about putting on a show after all."

"Yes, I suppose it's true that the show really must go on," I said.

"But wasn't the dead actress playing Dorothy?"

"Yes but there's another cast member who knows all the lines," as I said it, I nearly jumped out of my shoes. "Of course. Another motive." I was talking to myself. Franki looked rightly puzzled.

"Motive?" she asked.

I shook my head. "Ignore my wild woman ramblings. By the way, can you describe the two actresses who just entered the diner?"

She shrugged. "Young and talkative. One had white blonde hair. Oh, and one had on a jacket that Kylie nearly fell over herself asking about."

"A vintage bomber jacket?" I asked.

"That's it."

"Thanks, Franki. Enjoy your massage." I hurried off. I needed to read Nate's report and then hurry back to the diner. With any luck, I'd catch Joan and Carly still eating. I had a few questions about the cast, and they were always free with information.

I headed across Harbor Lane to the station. Hilda was busy on a dispatch call when I walked inside. She glanced up and continued talking but smiled and waved at me.

I paced rather anxiously in front of the counter until she finished the call. "Sorry about that, Lacey. Two important traffic signals went on the blink over in Mayfield, and they were causing all kinds of chaos. What can I do for you?"

"Actually, I talked to James and he told me I could look at the case report on his desk."

Another call came through but Hilda kindly buzzed me in before answering it. I gave her a silent thank you and headed into Briggs' office.

The worn leather chair sitting behind his desk smelled vaguely of his soap. I allowed myself a second to breathe it in before setting to work. Nate Blankenship's report was sitting right on top. The photos he took of Amanda at the scene were clipped to the front of the report. They weren't going to help my new quest because Amanda's face had been covered with stage makeup, the stage makeup that was, according to Constance, giving the actress a rash. It was the reason she gave for lending Amanda the Miracle Salve.

I skipped over the preliminary observations and flipped through to the details with the body graphics where Nate marked in areas where he discovered marks or wounds. Briggs was correct. The coroner was very thorough. Aside from the lacerations on her neck and fingers that were caused by the cable, he listed moles and bruises along with a small scar on her left arm that he determined resulted from an injury in childhood. There was no mention of any rash.

I sat back and thought about the night of Amanda's murder. I had been somewhat out of it with that rotten cold, but the first time I leaned over her and my nose neared her neck and face, I sneezed. At the time, I couldn't sort out what the out of place scent was but now I was convinced it was eucalyptus. It would explain my allergic reaction. So Amanda definitely had Miracle Salve on her skin but why? There was no rash. Constance had conveniently forgotten and then remembered that she lent the ointment to Amanda. Or maybe it got there a different way. Maybe it came off of Constance's hands when she held the cable around Amanda's neck. It was still thin evidence, but my intuition was pinging like a microwave timer.

I sat forward and thumbed through the report again. I skimmed through some of the science-y stuff and was rewarded for my efforts. Nate had swabbed the neck area, near the wound, and discovered a greasy substance that contained mineral oil, lanolin, glycerin and, naturally, eucalyptus oil. Nate had theorized that the victim was using some ointment to soothe dry skin, only I knew better.

I closed the file. I had everything I needed to bolster my theory. I needed to head across the street to the diner to talk to Joan and Carly. Something told me there was more to Constance's act of revenge than jealousy over a boyfriend.

Hilda was just writing a note for Briggs when I came back out of the office. She spun around on her chair. "That was fast. Did you find what you were looking for?" she asked.

"Yes I did."

"I'm just writing a few messages for Detective Briggs," she said. "Would you like to add anything?"

I was feeling pretty spunky and proud of myself. I decided to leave Briggs a cryptic message to see just how quickly he solved the case with my clue. "Yes, thanks, Hilda. Please write this 'Lacey says victim had no rash'."

Hilda wrote it quickly but then looked up in question. "Is that all? Will he understand what you mean?"

I smiled. "It might take him a minute, but I think he'll figure it out."

CHAPTER 33

One of Franki's daughters, Kimi, I was fairly certain because she wore bangs, greeted me the moment I walked into the diner. "Lacey, how nice to see you. Where would you like to sit?"

Kylie was taking an order at a nearby table. She took a second to wink *hello* then returned with pen to pad and a polite food server's smile on her face.

Everything in the diner seemed to be running smoothly. I hadn't expected anything else. Just like Elsie and her bakery, Franki's diner ran like a finely tuned machine. The twins would really have to mess up to put a hitch in the operation.

I scanned over the tables and spotted Carly's bleached white hair. "Actually, Kimi, I just wanted to talk to the two women at the table near the jukebox."

"The lady with the vintage bomber jacket? Kylie nearly dropped over dead when she saw it. It's not really my thing, but I guess it would look sweet with a pair of jeans. Go ahead then. They just got their bowls of chili and cornbread. Do you want some? I could order it special and bring it to their table."

"No, I'm fine but thank you for the offer."

I walked toward the table. Joan and Carly were deep in a conversation but I forged ahead.

Joan, the more talkative and friendly of the two, spotted me first. "Hey, Lacey, we sure do run into you a lot. Are you sure there aren't two of you?" She had a nice laugh at her joke.

"Actually, this meeting was intentional," I admitted. "I wonder if I could ask you two a couple of questions."

They exchanged perplexed looks, then Joan spoke for the two of them. "Sure, pull up a chair. We were just chatting and enjoying this unbelievably good chili. Best I've ever had. What about you, Carly?"

Carly was still trying to process why I'd sat down to talk to them. She didn't look nearly as eager as Joan to answer questions. Joan's foot jutted forward to lightly kick a response from her friend.

"Uh yeah, it's great chili. What kind of questions?" Carly's nose crinkled to let me know she didn't understand the reason for my visit.

"Jeez, Carly, why are you being so uptight? I'm sure Lacey just wants to know about opening night. It's set for tomorrow night at eight o'clock. We've been getting ready for it all day. Especially Constance. I mean, makes sense since she's taking over the big role and all."

Carly had loosened up now that she thought I was just there to ask about the play. "Yes and Connie has been a bear. Stay clear of her, if you know what I mean. Of course, she's excited as can be about getting to play Dorothy, but it's kind of stressful. It's been like a whole year since she played that part."

I perked up on my chair. It seemed I was going to be able to go right along with Joan's reasoning behind my unexpected visit.

"A year? Has Constance had to stand in for Amanda before? I

always knew that main characters had understudies in case they got sick or—"

"Died," Joan added. "Constance wasn't Amanda's understudy." It was Carly's turn to jut her foot out for a polite kick. Joan furrowed her brows at Carly. "What? It's no secret. Constance was a big name back then. She had lots of write-ups about her performance as Dorothy. And she was really good too. It's just that Amanda was better."

"Says who?" Carly chimed in. "That's a matter of opinion. I think Constance should have remained Dorothy. She's much friendlier and cheery like Judy Garland was in the movie."

"Yes but Amanda was much better at projecting her voice on stage. That was always Constance's biggest problem. Susie always had to yell at her to broadcast the lines for the audience and not just the actor standing next to her."

I followed their back and forth for a moment. The debate was rather moot since there was no chance of Amanda returning to the role. But something told me the details of how Amanda became Dorothy were going to enhance my murder theory greatly.

I rubbed my temple. "Let me get this straight. Constance used to be lead actress and Amanda was her understudy. Then their roles switched?"

Joan finished a bite of chili and closed her eyes to savor it before speaking. "Yes, it was a really a big deal at the time. Constance was devastated."

"And rightly so," Carly noted. "We were in New Jersey. Constance came down with a terrible flu two days before opening night. There was no way she could perform. Amanda was new to the group, hired as an extra. She didn't have a permanent part yet, but in her spare time she'd learned all of Dorothy's lines."

"Not just Dorothy's lines," Joan explained. "Amanda had graduated from some snooty private college with a drama degree. She was super smart. She memorized the lines for every main character. That way she figured she would have a main part anytime one of the lead cast members got sick or was called back home for an emergency or whatever."

Kylie stopped by the table. "Hello, Lacey, are you ordering?"

"No, thanks, I just stopped by to ask about the play."

"How are you guys enjoying the chili and cornbread?" she asked her customers.

"Divine," Joan said. "Beats my Uncle Ray's chili any day. But don't tell him I said that."

Carly rolled her eyes. "Sure, that's what she's going to do when she walks away from the table, Joany. She's going to grab her phone and text your Uncle Ray."

Kylie laughed. "I'll avoid the Uncle Ray phone call. Let me know if you need anything else."

"That reminds me," Joan said. "I've got to send my cousin a birthday gift. Do you think it's tacky if I just sent a gift card?" she asked Carly.

"That's what you always give me on my birthday," she reminded her. "It's nice but it doesn't exactly say 'I put a lot of thought into this'."

Joan shuffled on her seat and sat up straight. "That's what you always tell me to get you. You always say 'just get me an Amazon gift card, so I can pick my own gift'."

"That's because most people buy me things that I would never wear or use or ever pick for myself," Carly countered.

The momentary diversion had steered the girls away from the previous topic, and now, I felt as if I was intruding on a conversation between friends. Something told me it would be easy enough to pull them back to the Dorothy topic.

"I'll let you two finish your meal. It's good to know that there will be an actress with experience playing Dorothy on the stage tomorrow night."

Joan buttered some cornbread. "Yep. Constance played

Dorothy for eight months, and like I said, she was a great Dorothy. But then she got sick and Amanda stepped in. People thought she was outstanding. A couple of the producers happened to be in the audience that night, and they told Susana to switch the lead actresses. They wanted Amanda to be Dorothy. Constance was petite so she got moved to a Munchkin role. She plays a flying monkey some nights when we're short on extras."

"She must have been devastated when she lost that role," I said.

The girls exchanged glances.

"Who wouldn't be?" Carly said. "She quit at first but then she couldn't get parts so she came back to the group. But she hardly ever spoke to Amanda after that."

"That's a shame." I pushed up from the chair. "Well, enjoy the food, and I guess I'll see you two on stage tomorrow night."

Joan laughed. "We'll probably meet again since we keep running into each other."

"Lacey"—Carly's tone had turned serious—"if they haven't found the person who killed Amanda, do you think we need to be worried?"

It was a good question, and I had only one good answer at the moment.

"They haven't found the person yet, but my intuition tells me they're going to catch the culprit very soon."

"Really?" Joan nearly slipped off the front of her seat. "Who is it? Is it someone from the group?" She sat back with a pout. "Opening night is going to be ruined again"

I didn't have the heart to tell her that there probably wouldn't be an opening night. "Thanks for letting me sit in on your chili break. Take care."

"You too," Joan said as I walked out of the diner.

CHAPTER 34

$\mathcal{T}$he sun was setting on the horizon and the temperature was dropping fast. I crossed the street from Franki's Diner and headed to the town square. The temporary light poles that had been erected for the theater group's stay in Port Danby popped on as I reached the pathway to the square. I pulled out my phone for the umpteenth time, but there was no text or call from Briggs. It seemed I was on my own. Unfortunately, the distance from the diner to the town square was not nearly long enough for me to develop any kind of plan, so I was going to have to play it by ear.

I utilized the last few hundred yards of my trek to mentally list clues that were now forming a coherent case to prove Constance Jeeves killed Amanda Seton. Amanda had some of Constance's Miracle Salve on her skin, but I was certain she never asked to borrow it. Amanda did not have a rash from the makeup. The ointment got there somehow. Constance's hands could have easily transferred it to Amanda's skin during her struggle to strangle her with the cable. Constance was angry the day I saw her in the drug store. I could only assume that she had somehow gotten word that

Amanda and Gordon had been having a side fling. That would certainly be the final straw for an actress whose career suddenly took a major hit because she got the flu and her understudy stole the show and her lead role. But probably the biggest clue of all was that Constance had clumsily implicated Johnny Vespo as the killer by adding evidence after the murder. While she managed to commit the murder leaving very little evidence, her brazen attempt to frame someone else for her crime was not well thought out.

As I finished the thought, I caught a glimpse of Johnny's slicked back dark hair standing in the center of several of his coworkers. He was clearly agitated about something. I moved closer. He was absorbed enough in his rant to not notice me eavesdropping.

"Can't believe I had to go through an interrogation," Johnny said. His voice was slightly shaky and filled with rage. "Clearly someone was trying to frame me for murder. Thank goodness Billy was a witness. He knew my costume wasn't ripped. I handed it back in perfect shape."

"But who would do that to you, Johnny?" One of his small audience asked. Johnny was just tall enough to see easily over the circle around him.

Johnny's gaze caught mine. "Maybe it was you," he said angrily over the heads.

Everyone's face turned toward me.

"You're with that detective, that Briggs fella. He pulled me in for no reason at all. Maybe you ripped the costume to frame me." Johnny's nostrils were flared with anger.

I was caught off guard by the accusation. It seemed he was still stinging from my major rebuke on the wharf.

"What motive would I have to do that? I don't even know you. Although, there was that incident on the wharf," I added and looked around at the audience he'd held captive just a moment before. They looked back to him to see if he would tell them about the incident on the wharf.

He drew his mouth in tight. His face reddened. Apparently, he wasn't interested in explaining to his coworkers how he accosted a woman on the wharf and nearly forced himself upon her.

"What's going on, Johnny?" someone asked. "Why would this lady frame you for murder?" Their curious gazes turned far more suspicious.

"Did she kill Amanda?" someone asked.

Feet seemed to be discretely shuffling away from me.

"Oh my gosh, this is ridiculous." I walked forward and they retreated more. Johnny seemed pleased with what he'd started. His tight lipped expression took on a sinister grin.

"Look," I said. "I was waiting right outside that tent on Thursday night, dressed and polished for a night at the theater with my boyfriend." I looked pointedly at Johnny. "Detective Briggs. The first time I saw Amanda Seton was when she was dead on the stage floor." That statement made a few faces a shade or two paler. "I'm sorry to shock some of you but that's the truth. And while your friend Johnny deserves reprimanding for some of his behavior, he is not a killer. He has every reason to be upset because someone *was* trying to frame him for Amanda's murder."

Even though Johnny had just finished griping about it, a gasp made its way around the group as if it was the first time they'd heard it.

"Maybe that *boyfriend* of yours could finally catch the killer," Johnny sneered but his face was less red. He seemed somewhat pacified by what I'd said.

"I think that'll be happening sooner than you think." I might have been getting ahead of myself, but I was feeling more than a little confident that I'd solved the case.

I headed along the pathway, relieved to be out of that tense situation. I had a much bigger tense situation ahead of me.

I pulled my phone out and looked once more. No message from Briggs. He was obviously held up in some meeting in Mayfield. Since I'd walked through the town square so often in the past few days, there was plenty of activity and lots of faces that were slowly becoming familiar. Unfortunately, there was no sign of Constance.

I headed toward the trailers and was lucky enough to spot Susana. I had to make sure I didn't give away my true reason for showing up, yet again, at the town square.

"Oh my, you're here again," Susana said through nearly gritted teeth. It seemed no one was thrilled to see me. I supposed it was because I reminded them that something terrible had happened, and even though they were trying to get on with things and go about their daily business, Amanda's unsolved murder still loomed over them.

"Yes, I promise I won't get in the way. I was just looking for Constance. She had mentioned she had a very effective ointment for skin rashes. My floral assistant had an allergic reaction to some mint—"

"Miss Damon," a deep voice called from behind.

Susana looked past me and waved. "Yes, over here, Mr. Mayor."

My posture immediately crumpled, and I braced myself for another unwanted run in with the town's mayor. He hadn't noticed it was his least favorite Danby resident until I turned to look at him.

His ruddy, round face flattened. "Miss Pinkerton, what are you doing here? I'm sorry, Miss Damon, I can place some people at both sides of the town square to make sure people aren't wandering through and bothering you."

"I wasn't bothering her, Mayor Price," I snapped.

"Miss Pinkerton," he said huffily. "Bothering seems to be part of your nature. Now run along. Miss Damon and I have to discuss the details for opening night. You might not have noticed but these people are very busy getting ready for the show."

Susana seemed to take pity on me. She, of course, had no idea that Mayor Price disliked me immensely. "I think you'll find Constance in that first trailer with the green trim. She's practicing her lines for the Dorothy part. It is—" she paused. "It *was* Amanda's trailer."

"Thank you and good day, Miss Damon." I said nothing to the mayor as I spun around and headed to the leading lady's trailer.

CHAPTER 35

*a*rgh," I muttered as I looked at my phone. "Detective James Briggs, where are you?" I shoved my phone back into my pocket as I reached the trailer. I wasn't entirely sure what my plan was. I seemed to be winging it a lot lately, but the 'seat of my pants' thing had been working out.

A voice drifted through the open window of the trailer. It was Constance but she sounded funny. I passed up the steps and crept beneath the window to find out who she was talking to. With the words courage and heart being tossed about, I quickly realized Constance did not have a visitor. She was practicing her lines in a sing-song voice.

I paced a few minutes, suddenly a little uneasy about just walking in and starting up a conversation about murder. The Miracle Salve seemed like the best way to go. I took a steadying breath, headed up the steps to the trailer door and knocked lightly.

"Yes? Come in," she called still in her Dorothy voice.

The trailer, Amanda's trailer, was much more sumptuous than Susana's or the costumer's trailer. A plush green sofa bordered a thick rug. A sparkly crystal chandelier hung in the center of the space. Crisp white blinds hung over the windows and gold specked granite covered the counter beneath gleaming ash gray kitchen cabinets. There was even a professional stove set into the counter. Constance was at the far end of the trailer where a bedroom had been set with a pillow covered bed and a pretty walnut vanity cluttered with perfumes, makeup and jewelry. She was sitting on the satin stool in front of the three-piece vanity mirror.

"Did you remember the whipped cream on the coffee?" she asked before glancing over her shoulder. Her smile vanished instantly, then she forced it back onto her face.

"It's you. What are you doing here?" she asked. "I'm very busy learning my lines. I don't really have time to answer questions."

"Yes, I heard you'll be playing Dorothy now." I walked closer and stopped mid-kitchen, which was still just a few feet from where she sat. "I just came to ask you the name of the cream you were using. My shop assistant developed a rash on his hands while potting mint plants. I need to buy him some."

She looked greatly relieved at my question. (A little too relieved.) "Is that all? It's called Miracle Salve. Tell him just to rub it on the rash. It stings a little at first, but after a day, the rash will start to heal."

"So it takes a little time for the rash to disappear?" I asked.

"Well, yes, I mean obviously it's not instant," she said with a huff and turned back to her mirror. She picked up a shiny gold pair of earrings and held one to her ear. The lush surroundings were already going to her head. In her mind she was now lead actress, the star of the show, a title that had been stolen from her. Now she had deviously regained it.

"It's just that you mentioned you lent the cream to Amanda for a rash she got from the stage makeup," I said.

"Yes, that's right." She put the earring down briskly and twisted on the stool. "If you don't mind, I need to practice my lines."

"Of course. Sorry. I was just wondering about the Miracle Salve because the coroner didn't find any signs of a rash or skin irritation on Amanda. Other than the red marks left behind by the cable, of course."

Without turning around, she stared at me in the reflection in the mirror. Her lips rolled in and out, smearing some of her bright red lipstick on the skin around her mouth. Her bottom shifted haughtily on the satin stool. "Then I guess it really is a miracle salve." She shot a smirk by way of the mirror. "I must ask you to leave. I'm busy."

"Of course. Nice trailer, by the way. You have wonderful taste," I said.

"Please," she scoffed. "This place is like a little girl's princess bedroom. I'm going to modernize it just as soon as the new budget comes in."

I rubbed my hand along the top of the sofa. "I rather like it. But I guess I misspoke. I like Amanda's style. Since you two didn't get along, I suppose it makes sense you'd want to change it."

I could see every change in her demeanor and expression in her mirror reflection and her posture on the stool. Her back and shoulders were rigid with tension.

"That's just silly. Amanda and I got along just fine. What would you know about any of it anyhow?"

"You're right. I just thought because you were once cast as Dorothy and then Amanda took the role over that you might have held a grudge."

Even though I was hurtling some pretty strong stuff at her, she refused to spin around to face me and spoke to me, instead, through the mirror.

"Susana made a big mistake then but soon she'll see that she was wrong. I plan to shine on stage as Dorothy. Then everyone will see that I've always been a better actress than Amanda."

"I'm sure they will. Guess that's why you had to get her out of the way. How else were you going to prove to everybody that you were the true star?"

"Right," she said quickly, then shook her head. "No, wait, what are you talking about?" This time, she faced me but she remained seated. She pushed her hands between her knees to hide the fact that they were trembling. "If you don't leave my trailer, I'll call someone to come throw you out."

"If you say so." I meandered toward the door. "By the way, you might want to avoid Johnny. He's really angry about you trying to frame him. He was out there just now telling everyone how he got pulled into an interrogation room. Fortunately for him, he had a witness who could verify that the costume was in perfect shape when he handed it off to the costume department."

"No it wasn't," she snapped. "There was a large rip in the back where he ripped it on the house. You saw it. I showed you the costume and everything." Her face moved from red to grayish white then back to red. "You have gotten your nose in where it doesn't belong. You're just a busy body. Now get out of here before I call the police." She spun back to the mirror to let me know we were through talking. She fiddled with something on the vanity, but her body was turned at an angle that blocked my view. Fortunately, I could still *view* things through my nose. She had apparently taken the top off a bottle of perfume, a French brand. An expensive one with a hint of real jasmine.

I walked closer. "Maybe we should call the police. Then you can explain to them how you killed Amanda Seton. She stole your part in the play and when you saw her with Gordon—"

"She deserved the same end as the Wicked Witch." Her voice was low and odd. The tension in her body had dissolved into visible shudders. She shot up from the stool and twisted wildly around. I'd predicted her next step and covered my face and eyes before the expensive perfume reached me. What I hadn't anticipated was her violently shoving me back against the granite counter. The hard polished edge of the stone counter jammed painfully into my back. I instinctively shot forward and fell to my knees. When the pain had cleared my head and I was able to focus, a pair of ruby red slippers came into view.

My face shot up. Constance lifted a frying pan above her head. I reached forward and yanked hard on both her ankles. The red slippers flew off. She screamed as she fell backwards into the kitchen table. The frying pan clanged on the floor next to me.

I sprang to my feet and was suddenly blinded by the setting sunlight pouring into the trailer. A silhouette appeared in the doorway.

"Lacey," Briggs said frantically. His urgent footsteps shook the trailer as he raced toward me. Seconds later, I was in his embrace. The lingering pain on my back assured me I was going to have an ugly bruise. It seemed Constance would too.

She groaned and reached around to her back as she pushed to her knees. Her large eyes glared up at me. There was nothing about her face that seemed like the real Constance. She looked hard and vicious and truly wicked. "You stupid busy body," she sneered. "I was going back on stage. I was going to be Dorothy. You've ruined everything."

A few more footsteps rocked the trailer. Officer Chinmoor was followed closely by a bewildered Susana. A few of the other cast members peered around the edges of the doorway to see what was going on.

Briggs slowly released his hold on me, but I kept close at his side. "Chinmoor, arrest this woman for the murder of Amanda Seton."

An audible chorus of gasps followed. Gordon pushed himself past the others crowding the doorway. Briggs put up a hand to stop him from proceeding any farther.

"You killed Amanda?" The shock had caused Gordon's voice to crack. "You're crazy. I should have broken up with you long ago."

His words caused Constance to sob silently. Her shoulders shook as her entire life came crumbling down around her. She picked up one of the ruby slippers and stared at it. "I was supposed to be Dorothy. It was my part. It was always my part." Her words trailed off. If my back hadn't been throbbing in pain, I might almost have felt sorry for her.

"That's it," Susana said as she tried to herd the cast away from the door. "Show is off. Head back to your trailers and get ready to pack up camp. We're through in Port Danby."

I looked at Briggs. "The mayor is going to be so mad at me."

"Do you care?" he asked.

"Not really."

His nose crinkled up. "You smell good but strong. Making my eyes water."

"It's perfume. Expensive perfume if my nose is still as discerning as it was back in my perfumery days." I discretely reached for his hand. "I guess you figured out my clue, but it took you a little too long," I said. "I'm going to have a bruise on my back."

"If you're going to leave me an explosive clue that needs to be solved quickly to avoid you getting killed, then don't count on Hilda. I was in the office a good ten minutes before she came in and said Lacey had left a message, then another three minutes for her to remember what you said."

"Next time—" I started.

"No next time." He squeezed my hand and led me out of the trailer. The look on his face assured me a lecture would follow.

An enormous crowd of people had gathered to find out why police cars had pulled up to the town square. Members of the theater group were huddled in different places, no doubt discussing the alarming news. A few of the stage crew were already pulling large props out of the tent to begin the tear down process.

Briggs led me toward his car. He had pulled right onto the grass in front of the trailers. "Lacey, I've told you again and again not to confront killers. You could have been seriously hurt or worse." In between his fatherly scolding, he stopped several times to clear his throat.

"I know but Constance is several inches shorter than me—" My size matters defense was cut short by his sneeze. "Bless you."

"Thanks." He shook his head. "It doesn't matter if Constance is shorter and slighter than you."

I put up a finger. "Uh, I didn't say slighter. Just shorter."

He grinned faintly. "My mistake. It doesn't matter that she's shorter. Amanda Seton was a good five inches taller than Constance, and she still couldn't fight her off."

I nodded lightly. "I'm sorry and I won't do anything so foolhardy again."

He sneezed again.

I blinked at him for a second. "Uh oh, did I do that?"

"I've been trying to ignore the sore throat all day, hoping it would just go away."

I scrunched my face up. "Sorry."

"I'm only sorry I wasted all those kisses when I was going to get the cold anyhow." He leaned against his car. "So, how did you figure this one out, Super Nosed Sherlock?"

"I was having a tough time putting pieces together with this one, but it all had to do with Ryder being allergic to mint."

"I know this is heading somewhere that will eventually make sense."

"Yes it is. Ryder's rash reminded me about my chat with Constance about the Miracle Salve. At first she didn't mention lending any to Amanda until I brought up that Amanda had some on her skin. She wasn't terribly smooth about it all, but in her haste to fill in the story she said Amanda had developed a rash from the stage makeup so she needed the ointment."

"Ah, so that's why you needed to see the coroner's report. Nate would have listed any rashes on his report."

"Yep, good ole thorough Nate. There was no rash. I also found out that Constance used to play the role of Dorothy. Then she caught the flu and Amanda had to step in to cover for her. She was so good in the part, Susana made her the permanent Dorothy, and Constance was demoted to a Munchkin and flying monkey. It would be enough to make any budding actress upset. Even upset enough to kill. Especially when the person who stole your starring role was also attempting to steal your boyfriend. I think that Constance saw Amanda with Gordon and it pushed her last button."

Briggs nodded. "Impressive." He touched his throat as he swallowed. "A sore throat. Last thing I need."

I cuddled up against him. "I think what you need is a few days off to recuperate. And chicken soup. And fruit smoothies. And maybe some of Elsie's quinoa and vegetables. And some tender loving care from your girlfriend."

"I'll take everything, but I draw the line at quinoa. It doesn't even sound like it's edible."

I rolled my eyes. "You sound just like Les."

He kissed my nose. "Let me finish my job here, then you can meet me at my house with some of Franki's chicken soup and some of that tender loving care."

CHAPTER 36

*B*ear trotted up to me, instantly smitten. As much as I would have liked to think the longing look from his big brown eyes was for me, I knew it was for the container of Franki's chicken soup I held in my hand. Briggs was on his couch with a blanket around his shoulders and a box of tissue on his lap. It was so rare to see him weak and vulnerable that I almost wanted to take a picture.

"You poor guy, you've got the Rudolph syndrome." I stopped and gazed down at him. "But you're still my handsome prince despite the sallow complexion, dark under eye rings and bulbous red nose."

"Thanks. And good to know my nose is not just red but that it's grown into a bulb just like Rudolph's. Why was that, anyhow? I mean, sure he was born with a red nose, but why was it so enormously big as compared to the other reindeer?"

I laughed. "I see you've grown philosophical and deep in your sickness." I held up the carton of soup. Bear, who had sat obediently at my feet, lifted his head so his twitchy nose could follow the carton of soup and its dreamy aroma. "Should I heat some up and allow the miracle of Franki's soup to get started on the healing process?" I asked.

Briggs pushed himself deeper into the couch cushion and pulled the blanket tighter around his shoulders. "Not sure I'm in the mood for soup. A glass of orange juice sounds better."

"One glass of OJ coming right up." I carried the soup to the kitchen. Bear's feet clip clopped across the wood floor as he trotted behind me. He released a squeaky, doggy groan as I put the soup in the refrigerator. I spun around to him. "Don't worry, big guy, I didn't come empty handed." I reached into my coat pocket and pulled out two of Elsie's peanut butter dog treats. Bear's ears perked with glee as he took the treats from my hand and dashed off to enjoy them on his pillow.

I poured a glass of orange juice and handed it to Briggs before sitting down next to him.

He glanced sideways at me. "I think you're probably sitting in the germ space." He drew an imaginary line around himself.

"I think since I gave this germ to you originally, it has no chance of bouncing back to the giver. And don't I just sound like someone who had several years of medical school. My professors would be so proud." I relaxed back next to him. "Any news on Constance?"

"Just that you nailed everything. She was harboring a year long grudge for losing the Dorothy part to Amanda, and when she spotted Gordon cozying up to Amanda something snapped. She had been in Susana's trailer, complaining that the makeup was giving her a rash. Susana's phone was sitting on the table next to her laptop. She stuck the laptop cable in her pocket to be used as a murder weapon. She spotted a text conversation where Susana was asking Amanda to stay after dress rehearsal so they could talk. She knew Amanda would be in the tent, but she had to make sure she stuck around after Susana finished talking to her. She was mad at Gordon, so she decided to implicate him in her future crime by sending a text from his phone. Later she switched her ire to Johnny because Gordon had come back around." Briggs turned his face to me without lifting his head from the couch. "But none of her schemes worked because the amazing, relentless and clever Lacey Pinkerton was on the case."

"Uh, I believe you forgot adorable in your list of adjectives."

"Adorable is a given." He reached over and took my hand. "Thanks for your help, Miss Pinkerton. Couldn't have done it without you."

BANANA WALNUT MUFFINS

View recipe online at londonlovett.com/recipe-box

Banana Walnut
MUFFINS

Ingredients:

- 1½ cups all-purpose flour
- 1 teaspoon baking soda
- 1 teaspoon salt
- 1 teaspoon cinnamon
- 2 eggs (*or substitute 2 Tbsp ground flax + 6 Tbsp water*)
- ⅓ cup oil
- ¾ cup brown sugar

- 1 cup mashed ripe banana (2-3 bananas)
- ⅓ cup milk
- ⅓ cup chopped walnuts
- ⅓ cup mini chocolate chips

Directions:

1. Pre-heat oven to 350°. In a small bowl, mix together flour, salt, baking soda and cinnamon.

2. In a large bowl, mix together the oil, eggs (or flax eggs), mashed banana, milk and brown sugar until well combined.

3. Add the dry ingredients from the small bowl into the large wet ingredient bowl. Stir until just combined.

4. Fold the chopped walnuts and mini chocolate chips into the batter.

5. Prepare muffin pan by greasing or lining with muffin cups.

6. Fill each muffin cup two-thirds full with batter.

7. Bake at 350° for 24-28 minutes, until toothpick comes out clean.

8. Allow muffins to cool for a few minutes before transferring to a cooling rack.

9. ENJOY!

There will be more from Port Danby soon. In the meantime, check out my new Starfire Cozy Mystery series! Books 1-3 are now available.

Los Angeles, 1923. The land of movie stars and perpetual sunshine has a stylish new force to be reckoned with—**Poppy Starfire,** *Private Investigator.*

See all available titles: LondonLovett.com

ABOUT THE AUTHOR

London Lovett is the author of the Port Danby, Starfire and Firefly Junction Cozy Mystery series. She loves getting caught up in a good mystery and baking delicious, new treats!

Join London Lovett's Secret Sleuths!: facebook.com/groups/londonlovettssecretsleuths/

Subscribe to London's newsletter at www.londonlovett.com to never miss an update.

London loves to hear from readers. Feel free to reach out to her on Facebook: Facebook.com/londonlovettwrites, Follow on Instagram: @londonlovettwrites, Or send a quick email to londonlovettwrites@gmail.com.

Made in the USA
Monee, IL
25 November 2022

18503796R00118